Y   Peck

SPANISH HOOF

$11.99

48510

Jun14 '85	4809		
Jun28 '85	160		
Oct 11 85	4187		

Y   Peck   48510
    SPANISH HOOF

Jun14 '85

Jun28 '85
Oct 11, 85

De 27'85

DISCARDED

Hard times are nothing new to the Beechers of Spanish Hoof. Running a Florida cattle ranch is hard work, and the Depression just makes everything harder. But life is good. Sixteen-year-old Dab is in love, Harry has a new pony, and Mama is optimistic that this year's herd of calves will pay off the bank. Counting hired hands Poke and Lightning as family too, the Beechers have each other and their ranch: this is real prosperity.

But in the summer of her twelfth year Harry sees her world begin to change: her mother is getting older; her brother is looking to the future. Harry is sure it will be a long time before *she'll* fall in love or want to be called Harriet. Right now she's happy to be Harry, a kid with a pony. And then disaster hits Spanish Hoof. As the Beechers band together to save their ranch, Harry makes a decision that is as painful and inevitable as growing up.

As in his classic *A Day No Pigs Would Die,* Robert Newton Peck memorably portrays the solidarity of family and the end of childhood. Told with Peck's characteristic humor and simplicity, this poignant novel of a family's determination to keep its home will reach the hearts of all readers.

Books by Robert Newton Peck

Robert Newton Peck

SPANISH HOOF

Alfred · A · Knopf   New York

THIS IS A BORZOI BOOK
PUBLISHED BY ALFRED A. KNOPF, INC.

"Pretty Red Wing" by Martin Christian
Silverhill Music (BMI)—Copyright 1980
Used by permission.

———————————

Copyright © 1985 by Robert Newton Peck
Cover illustration copyright © 1985 by Wendell Minor
All rights reserved under International and Pan-American
Copyright Conventions. Published in the United States by
Alfred A. Knopf, Inc., New York, and simultaneously in
Canada by Random House of Canada Limited, Toronto.
Distributed by Random House, Inc., New York.
Manufactured in the United States of America

2   4   6   8   10   9   7   5   3   1

Library of Congress Cataloging in Publication Data
Peck, Robert Newton. Spanish Hoof.
Summary: The year she turns twelve on Spanish Hoof,
her family's beloved ranch in Florida, Harry gets a pony
and learns some hard lessons about life.
1. Children's stories, American.   [1. Ponies—Fiction.
2. Ranch life—Fiction.   3. Florida—Fiction]   I. Title.
PZ7.P339Su   1985   [Fic]   84-21776
ISBN 0-394-87261-4   ISBN 0-394-97261-9 (lib. bdg.)

Spanish Hoof is dedicated to the
hardworking woman of America,
who, often without a husband,
raises cabbages, calves, and children.

Robert Newton Peck

ACKNOWLEDGMENT

Robert Newton Peck wishes to
cheer his friend and
neighbor, Don Dizney, and
our favorite football team,
the Orlando Renegades.

ACKNOWLEDGMENT

Robert Newton Peck wishes to
cheer his friend and
neighbor, Don Dizney, and
our favorite football team,
the Orlando Renegades.

SPANISH HOOF

Chapter 1

"Hang on, Harry."

"I will," I yelled down to my big, bossy brother, Dab, who was standing far below me, next to the horse trough, under the tall tower of our windmill.

"And don't look down. If you do, ya might spin yourself dizzy and tumble," Dab hollered up at me.

Dabney was near to turning sixteen and knew it all. Or usual thought he did. I'd never climbed quite this high on our windmill before, and my hands felt a mite washy on the ladder rungs. Away off to the east I could hear the clang of Cheater's wagon.

He was winding our way. At last! I'd easy remember today forever. The tenth day of May, 1933.

The noise sounded a bit like a distant church bell, even though today wasn't Sunday. I figured what caused it. Cheater McCabe's wagon usual packed a store of tools and cooking gear that he dangled down on the outside. So the clang, clang, clang that I heard might be something like a hacksaw ringing a frypan.

"Can ya spot 'im yet?" Dab asked.

48510

"Nope. But I can certain see lots else."

"That's ample high enough, Harry. Ya know, if Mama catches you up yonder, she's gonna thump your bottom until it's redder than a radish."

"I'll risk it."

Squinting, I looked out across all of Florida, trying to locate Cheater's wagon through the gaps in the oaks, laurels, and fan palms that crowded the road from the town of Otookee all the way to Spanish Hoof, our ranch.

Dabney was yelling up at me again. "Cuss your fooly little hide, Harriet. I swear, if'n you shinny up one more rung, I'm climbing up there to snake you down."

Just because I was only eleven, I was thinking as I held tight to the gray wood, Dabney Beecher thought he was my boss. Well, he wasn't. Mama was the only boss of Spanish Hoof. Shading my eyes with one hand, I could see Cheater's two mules; and they certain were spending their sweet old time along the red sand of the road.

"He's coming," I hollered down. "But I sure do wish he'd trot his mules a lick, to hurry 'em along."

Cheater McCabe stopped here at Spanish Hoof usual about one trip a month. His real name was Chester, but some prankster had changed a letter in the name that was printed on his wagon. Leastwise, that was how Mama told it; and Cheater was too amused to change it back to Chester.

I couldn't see the peddler wagon, yet the clangs

were creeping closer and no longer sounded so painful distant.

Turning to look south, I saw Gertrude, our big
black Santa Gertrudis bull. He's a Spaniard, Mama
says. Years back, Florida was the first grassland in
all of America to get hoofbit by Spanish cattle. So
she named our ranch Spanish Hoof.

"Best you inch yourself down now, Harry. If'n ya
linger up yonder much longer, old Cheater'll be here
and git gone before *you* do."

I sure didn't cotton for that to happen. I started to
work my way down the long windmill ladder so that
I'd be smack to the ground and running by the time
Cheater moaned a whoa to his mules. After about
three rungs I spotted his wagon passing between the
pair of tall posts that straddled the road and held up
the sign that said SPANISH HOOF.

Dabney waited for me to land, whipping off his
cowboy hat to dust my rump with an easy swat.

"Dang you, Harry," he said. "Scamper into the
house and pull on a shirt. It ain't too ladylike to
greet callers when you're only half flagged."

All I had on was jeans and an undershirt. I hadn't
took the time to fuss myself fully dressed.

"Where's *your* shirt?" I asked.

Dabney let out a troubling sigh. "That's different," he told me. "I'm a man, in case you're too dull
to know what's which. So scoot inside and pull a
shirt on. Even though all you'll be hiding is dirt."

"I'm not doing it for *you*," I shouted over my

shoulder as I ran toward the house. "I'll do it to comfort Mama and for modest."

"Bring one for me too, Harry. Okay?"

"Sure," I answered. I felt extra social because it was May and school was over. Besides, today was a special event. Sometimes, on real important days, Mama made me wear a dress so's I'd look like who I honest was, Harriet Beecher. But not today. Grabbing the first shirt I could spy, I poked my head through its neck and then yanked out both my pigtails as I ran out the door. But not before I also grabbed a shirt for Dabney, as Mama didn't want either one of us to meet callers with a bare chest.

"Let's go, Harry," Dab yelled to me. "Unless you're not interested in what Cheater's hauling behind him."

We ran. Dab was pulling his shirt on; but even so, his longer legs ate up the sand quicker than mine could, yet I near to kept up.

Cheater McCabe's rig didn't actual look like a regular wagon. It was more like a moving junkpile. The clanking of his tools and utensils rattled worse than a factory. But to my ears, on this day it whistled out sweeter than Christmas music. Lots of other times, when Cheater arrived at Spanish Hoof, I'd run out to greet him and then jump up to share the seat bench so's I could ride up to our house in real peddler style.

Not today.

What I knew Cheater McCabe was bringing

wasn't inside his wagon among all the bags of salt, flour, and sugar, the rolls of cloth, the tools, and such. I sped myself past the turning wheels and pulled up sudden.

"There's your pony, Harry," said Dab.

Looking at him for the very first time, I couldn't move or speak.

My heart was half laughing and half crying. All to one pump. The pony was haltered at the tail end of a ten-foot lead rope, trailing between the shallow ruts fresh-dug by the wagon's wheels. He was spotted brown and white, a whole lot prettier than all my dreaming about him ever painted up.

He didn't trot. He danced. Four creamy hoofs kicked the red sand and stitched it into a long sewing seam. As the lead rope dipped slack, the pony turned his beautiful face to look at me with eyes browner than a pair of wet pecans. Then he tossed his head as if to throw me a howdy.

"Well," said Dab as the pinto trotted by me, "say something, Harry, now your mouth's yawned open."

But all I could manage was breathing, and I honest had to force my lungs to handle even that. As Dab and I followed along beside the pony all the way up to the house, I listened to the clang, clang of Cheater's hardware mixed in with the thumps of my heart.

Cheater reined in his mules.

Then I saw Mama riding around the corner of our

barn, hurrying like usual. I'd never seen my mother ever tackle a job slow. Mama kicked off her horse before he'd even pulled to a whoa.

Cheater stood up quick and took off his hat, to respect Mama, even though she always wore trousers. Except to church. "Howdy do, Violet," he called out. "As y'all can see, I brung a ugly critter for your daughter." Cheater took his time climbing down off his wagon seat, stepping on a wheel spoke, then to the sand. He bowed to Mama, real courtly, as he always did. "Violet Beecher," he said, "you just seem to grow prettier every month. I swear holy you certain do."

"Hush, you handsome rascal," said Mama, "and shake hands with me. I got cow dust on my fingers, so I'm itched to wipe it off on somebody."

Cheater grinned, showing his yellow teeth. "Violet," he said serious, "there ain't any prouder dirt in all of Florida."

Mama sighed. "Tell that to the Otookee Bank."

Chapter 2

I hugged Mama.

"Come see." Yanking her hand, I pulled her around to the rear of Cheater's wagon so she could feed her eyes on my pony.

As she looked Mama rested her hard fists to skinny hips. Then she shook her head, smiling in a pleasing way. "Ya like him, Harry?" she asked me in a soft voice.

"Oh," I said, "if I liked him even a speck more, I'd just swelly up and bust."

"He looks prime and pretty," Mama said.

"You do too," snorted Cheater. "A flower of a woman like you, Violet Beecher, oughtn't to reside a ranch away out in the Everglades with no husband. I'd wed ya sooner than Sunday."

Mama smiled. "That's an honor, Chester. But I had me a husband, years back. And my Clarence Beecher was the best man in Florida. Thanks for the offer, but I rest happy in my memories."

Cheater and Mama always talked wed talk. Every month. It was a game they played, and everybody knew it was ear high in josh. They didn't look at each other in the manner that Dab eyed Trudy Sue.

Trudy Sue Ellsworth lived most of four miles south of us. The Ellsworths were our nearbyest neighbors. I'd long ago noticed that whenever Trudy Sue rode her sorrel over to Spanish Hoof, my brother would hustle to slick down his hair. Then he'd hook thumbs into his belt and strut to greet her as though he was a full-growed rancher.

Watching the two of them serpent around in the shade and giggle was enough to reverse my stomach. And the expression on Dabney's face could near to choke a chigger.

Behind me, I heard our kitchen door squeak open. *"Yahoo!"*

Hearing his holler, I turned to see Poker busting out the kitchen door, limping our way on his stiffy old leg. Like customary, Poke was wearing his stained apron, and in one of his hands he toted a long stirring spoon.

"Howdy to ya, Poker," said Cheater. "I fetched in the flour and sugar you ordered on the last visit."

Poke snorted. "Howdy back. But I'm too excited to trade. I gotta see me Harry's new pony."

"There he is." I pointed.

Poke waggled his long spoon to circle the air. "Bless a boot, Harry. He's a beauty." The old man who did our cooking gave me a squeeze, and I squeezed him back, inhaling Poke's customary smell, a blend of coffee, grease, and stove smoke.

Before I could wiggle loose, Poke grabbed me by the seat of my jeans and planted me smack on my pony. "There," he grunted. "How's he feel, Harry? Does he fit under ya snug as cozy?"

"Snugger," I said.

Lightning come to join us, taking his time. His freckled face bent me a grin. He was our hired cowhand and was sort of the opposite of Mama. He wouldn't hurry if both his feet were on fire. But he tackled his work. Mama always mentioned that she hoped someday to discover exactly what Lightning was saving up energy for. She said it certain had to be one special event, and she sure didn't aim to blink and miss it.

"Violet," said Cheater, "you told me not to bring no saddle, so I didn't fetch one with me. But seems like your little gal here deserves one."

Mama clucked at him. "The saddle will have to wait patient. I'll be lucky if I can unfold enough presidents to trade for the pony. Times are tough, Cheater."

Cheater winked. "Times always was, Violet."

Mama slapped her leg. "Reckon so. Part of the Lord's plan, as I figure it. That way, the weaklings die off."

Everybody crowded around to unhitch the pony. I saw Dabney keep a tight hold on the lead rope, as if he thought I was too little to go gallop off on my lonesome and then slipper off to eat cactus.

"Best we unload," said Cheater.

Poke and Lightning each grabbed a white sack, one flour and one sugar. Lightning helped himself to the lighter one, the sugar. His doing it didn't escape Poke's eye.

"Shirky," Poke grumbled.

Lightning and Poke usual pretended they were born enemies. Yet they mostly were teasing at each other. I could hear Poke cussing away at Lightning, who was laughing, all the way until they both disappeared through our kitchen door.

"Harry," said Mama, coming over close to where I sat on my warm new pony, "you'll have to think up a fitting name."

"Sure enough," I told her. Yet he'd deserve a special name. Something grand.

"Say," said Cheater, waving his hat in the air, "I brung along my box Brownie. If'n you want my opinion, today'd be a smacker of a time to print up a camera portrait of the Beecher family. Pony and all."

Mama looked at her clothes. "Chester McCabe, you sure do have a talent for timing, just because I never stunk dirtier in my entire life."

Dab smiled. "Ma, a camera can't *smell.*"

Mama howled out a laugh. "No, son, I don't guess it do. Okay, we'll crank her up. Dabney, run up to the house and fetch back Lightning and Poke. And tell 'em to quit scrapping long enough to pose." Cheater already had fished his Brownie camera, a black box, out of his jumble of wares and was fiddling with a dial. Mama took off her floppy hat and raked a red bandana over her face. "S'pose I'll do," she said. Her smile widened as her hand brushed some grit off my cheek.

"You look beautiful, Mama," I said.

"Do I, Harry?"

I nodded. "And nobody'll have to spur *me* into a smile. Not today. I'm so joyous happy I could pop like red corn."

Dabney come back with Lightning and Poke. We all huddled together—me on my pony and the rest standing stiller than stones. My nose smelled something fancy. Poke had slapped some store-bought pomade on his hair. Looking closer, I could tell that he'd also added a squirt or two on Lightning's curls.

"Ready?" asked Cheater, adjusting the legs of his tripod into loose sand.

"Fire away," Mama told him. "We all might not look to be fancy much, but we're all we got."

I saw Lightning slide a step to his left so he'd stand exactly in front of Poke. Our old cook grunted a protest. Dabney smoothed a scattery lock of Mama's graying hair. As I softly patted my pony I felt really proud of our family. All five of us. I sure was a lucky kid.

"Smile," ordered Cheater from underneath the raggy old cloth that was now quilting his head and one shoulder.

"Hold it," I called out.

Dab sighed. "Now what's wrong?"

13

"Maybe," I said, "we ought to get Gertrude to pose in the picture too."

Cheater popped up from under his photographer's shawl. "Gertrude? Who in the blazes is *she?*"

I saw Mama bend a smile.

"He's our new Santa Gertrudis bull," she said. "Maybe, considering our calf crop he's been producing, he's the whole blessed future of Spanish Hoof." Mama sighed. "I got me a breeder bull named Gertrude and a daughter we handled Harry. Puny wonder why folks in Otookee think I've wandered myself off the road."

"No," I told her. "They all respect you, Mama."

She squeezed my hand.

Chapter 3

Cheater McCabe went clanking off.

Next month, he'd told us as he was turning his wagon, we would see the picture that he snapped.

"Dab," said Mama, "you best help Harry turn her animal out to meadow. And right sudden. We got ample work to handle."

"You bet," said my brother.

Poke went limping over to the house, heading back to his kitchen where he'd continue to cuss at the stove.

"Then," said Mama, "you know where to find Lightning and me. You come along too, Harry. There's been enough pony for one morning."

"Sure," I said.

I knew better than argue. So I slid off my pony with a regretful sigh. During a workday, whenever Mama barked out an order, the rest of us hopped on it righteous pronto, like a rooster to a cricket. Mama kicked up into her saddle without hardly toeing a stirrup. Lightning mounted a bit slower. The two of them rode off.

"Let's do it, Harry," said Dab.

We pulled the rope halter off my pony and Dabney slapped him free. I itched to ride him more. Yet I knew not to whine about it. I also preferenced to help out Poker in the kitchen than do what had to get done with the calves.

"Come on," Dabney told me.

He untied his bay gelding, Socky, swung aboard, and then hefted me up behind him. I stretched my arms around the hard of Dab's skinny chest so's I wouldn't tumble. As he kicked the bay into a canter I leaned my face against the back of his checkerboard shirt. And then, closing my eyes, I pretended it was my pony I was riding.

Even before we got to the calf pen, I heard the noise of the place. All our brood cows were outside, bawling for their calves. And the calves were bawling back for their mothers. It was the first time they'd got parted.

A hot-iron smell crinkled my nose.

As we climbed off the gelding, under oak shade, Dabney railed the reins, and we went to join Mama and Lightning. The fire was already smoking, and Mama had her table set up with all her tools in line.

"Send 'em through, Dab," she said.

Dab and I poked the calves, one to a time, into the feed chute. The first calf reached the rack and bawled worse'n fury as his head got bar-locked near Mama's work area.

He sure was a balky little devil. Coal black, like

all our cows. I saw a cow cut away from the herd and approach as close as she dared, and I figured it was the calf's mother.

"Hyah!" Mama spooked the cow back with a wave of her hat, and Lightning talked to the frighted calf as if telling the little guy a bedtime story. It sure was plain to see why Mama kept Lightning as a hired hand at Spanish Hoof. He was slow, gentle, and church-quiet; and Mama always said she'd never witnessed no better hand at animals.

The calf bawled and tried to kick fearful as he took castrating, branding, and his ear notch.

I didn't like to watch.

The stink of it almost hurt worse than the sight. Mama burned a red-hot SH into his black fur until it hissed smoke. But then Lightning hit him with water. We used three branding irons. While one was smoking into hide, the other pair was roasting their heads in the fire ash. Mama said that maybe someday we'd brand cold, using liquid nitrogen that she'd heard would be less painful.

Lightning was crooning to the little bull calf that wasn't ever going to grow up to be a bull. He was now a steer.

"You're my baby," he sang, "healthy loud. Grow up happy and grow up proud."

As I worked alongside Dab, poking the animals into the chute one by one, I was ample glad that Lightning could sing so sweet to our calves. There was something about pain and hurting, anybody's, that nudged Lightning into making music. His song moved about as slow as he did. Yet it somehow sounded out proper.

"There ya go," Mama said to the calf, giving him his vaccination needle. "And bless your heart, youngster. Turn him loose."

Lightning had eased away the head bar to let the calf go limping and bleeding into freedom. He ran straight to his mama, bawling every step. She licked him. Then the two of them, mother and son, trotted away to shade.

I stayed outside the calf pen and up on the rails. Using a pole, I prodded the next customer along the chute to where Mama and Lightning waited with medicine, fresh heat, and more music. It was amazing to me how quickly they handled the job.

"Git," I ordered the calf.

Our herd of Black Angus brood cows kept their distance. But each cow seemed to know when *her* calf was getting its head locked at the far end of the chute. She'd break from the herd, snort, stamp a hoof, and bawl to her youngster. I never could reason how the mother cow knew, but she certain did.

"If I was a cow," I yelled to Dabney, "I don't guess I'd allow my calf to get branded and cut so hurtful."

Dab snorted. "Is that so."

"I'd take my calf and head off into the swamp where nobody'd find us," I said. "That's what I'd do."

"Until you'd met up a gator. Then you'd parade yourself right back home again."

Dab had climbed over the railing and was inside the calf pen, feeding the calves one by each into the mouth of the chute. I could barely see him because of the dry-spell dust that the calves were hoofing up.

"Gators don't spook me," I said.

Dab looked up and spat. "Harry, a person who don't respect a gator is about as leak-brained as somebody who don't respect a bull."

The calf Dabney was tussling with, a stocky four hundred pounder, bucked at Dab and pressed him against the fence rails. Dab didn't quit. Instead, he headed the black rascal my way, where I could prod him into the chute.

It wasn't too easy to talk. The calves never seemed to let up bawling. Whenever they'd quiet, the brood cows would take over. Not a single one, mother or calf, sounded even a mite content.

"Keep 'em coming," Mama yelled to me.

A rail slipped out from its nest in a post, dropping to the dirt. One calf spotted liberty and ducked out of the pen. Dab righted the fallen rail, vaulted over, and was polishing his saddle before you could swat a bug. I had to admire how fast Dabney rode down the calf, hazing him back toward the gate. Leaning my pole, I jumped down to crack the gate enough to crowd the calf back into the pen. Then I latched it nifty quick.

"Dang you, Harry." Dab slid off his horse and

shook my shoulder with a dirty hand. "Don't you never expose yourself that close to a spooked calf. Swing the gate clear open and hide behind it."

I climbed up a rail. "He's a baby."

Dab cuffed my fanny with his hat. "*Baby?* That animal could be near to a quarter ton, and that's just standing still. Charging into ya, he's double."

I looked around.

Mama was standing next to me, sweaty wet, holding a hot iron in one glove; in the other, she gripped her tongs. She didn't speak. But I could see her eyes looking my way out from under the brim of her battery old hat. Mama didn't look too pleasured that she'd seen me do foolish.

"Harry," she said, "I'd rather lose me a calf than lose me a daughter that I'm real fond of."

"Yes'm," I said.

Chapter 4

"He's the final," said Mama.

Lightning grinned. Lifting the bars of the holder, he let the last branded, castrated, and vaccinated calf go wobbling back to his big black mama, who had been pawing a hoof for him.

Dabney and I had walked over to the far end of the chute, while Mama was packing up her calf tools.

"Herd looks prospering," she said. "With luck, we'll satisfy the bank. I'm glad we traded off Ajax and got Gertrude instead. With a Santa Gertrudis bull servicing all our Angus brood cows, Spanish Hoof'll have a no-mix crossbreed."

"I'm glad we kept one bull calf," said Dab.

Resting her tools in the wagon bed, Mama leaned on a wheel. "Soon as he's matured, we'll let him breed us a few three-quarters, just to chart against our halfbreeds."

Dab and Lightning picked up the table to hoist into the wagon tail. I helped Mama wipe blood off her tools. The calf blood had a strong animal smell.

As I worked I noticed that there was more stain to Mama's shirt and trousers than on her utensils.

"No!" she yelped at me. "Don't never touch a branding iron, Harry." As she'd hollered, my hand was under an inch from it. I touched the handle and let it go even quicker. It felt plenty hot.

Dab shook his head. "Harry—"

"I know," I told them. "I'm a limit. But I was only fixing to help out, that's all."

Mama inspected my hand. Her gloves rubbed hotter than noon. So did her face. She stunk of calfing and sweat, but I didn't mind. It was how Mama usual smelled.

They let me drive the mule.

Her name was Golly. Poke bought her in Otookee one night when he'd tanked into some beverages, as he told it, with more personality than ginger ale. Poke rode her all the way home to Spanish Hoof. It had, he'd recalled to us, taken him most of the night to get here because he'd kept on falling to sleep and tumbling off her back. Golly, according to Poker, always waited for him to get up and climb back aboard.

"You're a good old lady," I told Golly, my fingers holding the leather ribbons as I sat the wagon bench.

The overhead sun warned us that it was nighing noon, so I figured that once we got back to the barn, Mama would seek out some shade under her favorite oak tree. It was where she liked to sit, lean, and rag off her sweat. Yet I was wrong.

"Boys," she said to Dab and Lightning, "let's tackle the tubs before Hoolie gets here with his load."

On the south side of our barn we'd stored three old bathtubs for several weeks. Poke had bought them in Otookee too, for a dollar each, and had hauled them home on the wagon. Nobody had told me why. I couldn't wait to see what was going to happen. Maybe Dab, Mama, and Lightning were fixing to fill these old tubs with pumpwater and take baths. This I certain had to view up close.

The three of them looked dirty enough, after chuting through all our beefs, to need a dozen baths each.

"I don't want a bath," I said. It was a big mistake. Because Dab and Lightning just passed a look between their eyes, loaded up with devil, and grabbed me.

"Mama!" I screamed.

"Use soap," she hollered back.

Below our windmill sat a water trough, with bugs in it; some swimming and others sunk. A few of the bugs were almost bigger than me, yet it didn't whoa Dab or Lightning. Neither did my scratching, kicks, or bites.

They ducked me. I called both of them a few fancy names that I'd picked up listening to Poker argue with our kitchen cookstove, using one or two of his saltiest old favorites. As I spat 'em out, Dab and Lightning kept dunking me until, they told me, my language got washed off to decent.

The Florida summer dried me.

"Let's load," Mama was saying. "Keep one tub here."

I still couldn't figure out what the old bathtubs were for. Maybe not, I was starting to reason, for the three really dirty folks who were loading them up and onto the wagon bed, behind Golly.

"Where y'all going?" I asked.

"Harry," said Dab, "quit your doggone pestering. Either help out or plug up that open hole under your nose."

I got to drive Golly again; and this time, Lightning and Dabney sat on the bench too, with me in the middle.

"Where to?" I asked them.

"Otookee," said Dab. "Me 'n' Lightning have had it with cattle ranching, so we're fixin' to start up a bathtub business in town." Dab pointed toward Otookee and clucked to Golly.

We headed down the red of the road.

"I don't believe you two birds," I said. "We're certain not going to Otookee, are we?"

Behind my shoulders, I could sort of feel how busy their eye-winkers were. I was hoping they'd fall off the bench and land on a hill of fire ants.

But we didn't really head far toward Otookee. Instead, Dab guided my ribbons to nose Golly and the wagon to the south meadow and over toward where the brood cows were licking their calves.

"Now what?" I asked them.

Dabney sighed. "I don't know how to tell ya this, Harry, but your job's to give each calf a bath."

"Me?"

Lightning nodded. He and Dab hopped down off the wagon. Inside, I still hunched they both were out to sport me, yet I went along with it. Golly let out a bray, as if she was efforting to tell me I was in for another prank.

"Well," Dab asked me, "which calf do you aim to give the first bath to?"

I squinted. "There's no water," I said, watching Dab and Lightning pull the first empty tub down off the wagon tailgate. The tub's feet thudded the sand and kicked dust.

Dab nodded. "Right. So there's only one thing to do when there's no water to bath a calf in."

I squinted at my brother. "And what's that?"

"Well," said Dabney, "ya gotta *spit* into a tub until it's full up. So start spitting, Harry, so's we can git done."

I wasn't about to fall for that.

"Hey! Here comes old Hoolie," said Dabney.

Hoolie Swain sometimes was a blacksmith and at other times worked for Mr. Dwayne Ellsworth, in his groves. Sure enough, Hoolie was coming with two mules and a wagon, pointed our way. As he came closer, I could see what kind of a load he was hauling. It was mostly a mix of white and orange and smelled like citrus pulp.

"This'll fat them calves," said Hoolie.

He was on the fat side himself, which sort of poked me to wonder if Hoolie Swain ate a lot of orange pulp. The way his belly lipped over his belt made me figure that he sure had worked his table fork. He was husky all over.

Hoolie got paid and left.

That was when Dab and Lightning tossed me into one of the tubs filled with citrus pulp and buried me until I was a sticky orange mess.

"That," said Dab, "is for all your unholy language."

Chapter 5

"Lord, please bless our food," Mama said. "Amen."

Soon as she said the "Amen," I saw Dabney snake out his fork to spear the biggest ear of corn.

"Manners," warned Mama.

Dab sighed. Yet he didn't put it back.

We sat in the kitchen around our big circle of a table. The five of us always ate supper as a family. Poker made sure to sit between Dabney and me so's we wouldn't punch at each other. Lightning sat next to Mama.

"Didn't turn out so good," Poke snorted.

It was what he often said, no matter what flavor of food graced the table, or greased it, because he hoped the rest of us would argue. He wanted to hear how tasty it all was when it hit our tonsils.

"Poker," said Mama, "if it swallows half as good as it smells, it'll be Heaven."

I noticed Poke's grin.

My steamy corn ear was starting to drip butter, so I licked it off. Mama caught me.

"Harriet, behave."

"I'm not Harriet," I said. "I'm Harry. You know that's what I like to get called."

Mama twisted her chicken wing. "A young lady who licks her corn ear just might get called Harriet ample often."

"Yes'm," I said, trying to be polite so's I'd be allowed to ride my new pony after supper.

As I chewed I watched Dabney pig in his meal. My brother could chomp away an ear of corn, end to end, faster than Poke could blow a scale on his harmonica.

There were two chickens on the platter, but neither one lasted too long. I put away all of my share. Mama took all four of the wings, even though I never could reason out why. Wing meat, the way I figured it, didn't taste near as juicy as the white.

"It's right good," Dab said to Poke. "Best buzzard you ever burnt."

Mama wiped her mouth. "Poke," she said, "if'n it weren't for you, we'd mostly starve. Or thin down to poor."

Poke grinned. "Thanks, Miz Beecher."

"I can handle most every chore on a ranch except a kitchen and a cookstove," said Mama. "Back when Clarence and I first got wed, I told my man that I'd do anything except fry or nag."

"Honest?"

Mama nodded. "As a young girl I made up my mind that I wasn't fixing to spend my life roped up to a sink. Not when there's the sweet outdoors and all of God's good Florida."

Lightning's plate was still near to halfway full. He was slow at eating too, even though he wasn't much older than Dabney.

I saw Mama smile at him. "Lightning," she said, "I swear, you're the only member of this family who *chews*."

Milk dribbled out of my mouth as I laughed and choked all to once.

"Swallow it," Dab said. "Don't breathe it."

As I was still busy trying not to drown, Lightning gently patted my back with his hand. "You got a milk moustache," he told me.

I grinned. "I got a pony too." That made everybody smile. "Before the sun backs off," I said, "I don't guess he'd mind if I rode him some."

"I'll go along with her," Dab said.

"No!" I yelled at him. "I aim to try it alone. And I certain don't need *you* to boss it all."

Poke scowled at me. "Harry, maybe you better go it soft at your pony, just to first. So's the two of ya can hatch friendly."

Mama nodded. "That's fair advice. Your new pony's in a strange place, and he might spook frisky. Dabney, you best slip a lead rope to his head for a day or so."

"I will, Mama. Unless ol' Harry aches to fly solo and learn how 'er rump can kiss the prickers."

Since Mama didn't chime in about my riding alone, I knew better than to kick up another fret.

After supper, the three of us Beechers wandered outside. Back in the kitchen, Lightning and Poke churned up a bicker about what order the dishes got washed. Poke was doing the bull share of ordering. He called himself King of the Kitchen; so, between the stove and the sink, he was boss. He also kept house for us and rearranged the dust.

I heard the kitchen door open. It was Lightning. Flashing me a grin, he tossed me a raw carrot. "A treat for your pony," he said.

"Thanks," I told him.

Lightning nodded and then disappeared back inside the kitchen.

Dab stood at the door of the shed, coiling a rope. "Come on, Harry," he said.

The two of us headed out onto the south meadow.

"There he is." I pointed.

My pony hadn't drifted too distant. Head lowered, he was chawing on fresh grass, inching his way along Florida, moving a hoof now and again. When he heard Dabney and me coming, he looked up.

"Hold it right here," said Dab.

"Why?"

"Well, maybe if you offer him a carrot, he'll come to you. That way, he'll begin to smart up that he's *yours*. And you're his."

"Come along, boy," I said, holding up the carrot so he'd see it.

"Now," said Dabney, "he's smelling. See his nostrils flare? So stand yourself still and let him walk to you in his own sweet time."

Taking the carrot from my hand, Dab cracked it into three shorter logs.

"I want to feed him," I said.

"Easy. You will." He handed me the three orange hunks.

I put two in my pocket and held the other on the flat of my open hand. I knew not to finger it because I figured ten fingers weren't too many.

"He's not coming very fast."

"Oh, he'll come. Ya gotta chat to him, Harry. Then, as he listens up to the stroke of your voice, he'll realize that every time he sees you, or smells and hears ya, he'll get something good. Like a carrot or a rub."

The pony just looked at us. I started to step forward, but Dabney's arm shot out to hold me back.

"Harry, hold quiet. Let him come to us. If'n it takes him an hour to do it, then accept it. Ya can't worry at him."

"Okay," I said.

Dab whistled. No sooner than he'd done it, I saw his bay, Socky, coming toward us at an easy trot. The gelding's one white sock climbed about fetlock high. My brother never moved. He just stood silent and let Socky hang his soft head over Dab's shoulder as if he wanted to welcome us to his meadow. Dab rubbed his face.

Watching it sort of grated me some. I wanted my pony to come to me the way Socky did to Dabney.

Dab grinned. "See?"

Socky nickered softly.

"S'matter, boy?" Dab asked him. "I bet ya smell

carrot on my hands, don't you? Well, that old carrot belongs to my sister."

That was all Dabney said. He didn't ask. Yet I caught him looking my way as if he was prompting me a mite.

I shrugged. "Okay," I said, giving two of the three carrot hunks to Dab. "Socky ought to get twice as much because he worked today, herding our calves."

Dab smiled. "You're a good one, Harry. If Socky could talk, I bet he'd tell ya thanks."

Right then I took a real surprise when I saw Dab feed one of the carrot logs to his horse and then chomp the other one himself.

I punched him. "Hey," I said, "they was both supposed to go to Socky, not *you*."

Dab laughed fit to busting. He sure did enjoy outsmarting me at every turn. But looking at my pony, with all of his brown and white patchwork, I sure couldn't stay sore for more than a breath or two. He certain was a handsome little guy, even though he was several sizes smaller than Socky. Ears up, he stared at Dabney and me as if wondering who we were.

"He likes his new home," I said.

"Well, he oughta," said Dab. "I figure that here on Spanish Hoof is about the best place in all Florida to live. Maybe even the whole world."

"I want to ride him. Right now."

Dab nodded. "Oh, you will. See? He's smelling your carrot again. A pony knows what's a honest treat."

Bending forward and stretching out my arm, I held the last hunk of carrot as close to my pony as possible without advancing toward him. "Right now," I heard Dabney tell me in a low voice, "that new pony of yours is about as curious as a dozen cats."

"Will he come?"

"Yup. Hearing our voices oughta help him decide. But it'll be *your* voice that'll fetch him, not mine. After all, he's your animal."

Waving the stubby piece of carrot, I said, "Come on, boy. And don't be bashful. It's just me—Harry."

To help matters out a mite, Dabney retreated some, taking Socky along with him.

"Please come," I told my pony.

It took about a hundred years of urging, but then the pony final made up his stubborn little mind. With a slight toss of his head, he walked slowly in my direction, nostrils flaring, like he wanted a carrot more than he wanted me for a friend.

"I'm your pal," I said.

He kept coming until I could feel his velvety lips reaching into my hand to pull the carrot into his mouth. Then I could hear his teeth munching it. Slowly I reached out a hand and patted him as gentle as I dared so's he wouldn't spook away.

"He's yours," Dab told me.

Chapter 6

"Can I ride him now?"

"I don't guess we can think of any sound reason why ya shouldn't. Bring him over to me."

Turning to Dab, I whispered, "How?"

"Well, while his mind's on the carrot he's still tasting, ease your arm under his chin and up the yonder side, like part of you is a halter."

As I did it, his neck and head felt wonderful warm.

"Now walk," Dab told me. "He'll follow along because he already cottons to feeling you so friendly and nearby. Maybe he's beginning to reason that you belong to him the way he belongs to you. Besides, the carrot juice on your hand'll make ya smell a lot more attractive than usual."

I ignored my brother's remark. Happy as I was right now, it didn't make a mite of sense to throw dirt at him.

"Keep him coming, Harry." When I started to quicken my pace, Dab added, "But there ain't no cause to rush matters. Sort of pretend that you're Lightning."

As Dabney advised, I eased my pony along, pretending I was Lightning, who worked, according to how Mama described it, at about one step ahead of whoa.

"Bring him to me," Dab ordered. "That's good. Now I can slip a loop of rope around his neck so's he don't git up a notion to bolt."

What I wanted to tell Dabney was that I itched to ride my pony all by my lonesome, without his bossing. Instead I held quiet. But this didn't set with Dab no better.

"Talk to him, Harry. Ya gotta learn to stroke an animal with your voice as well as your hand."

"That's it, boy," I told the pony. Looking at Dab, I said, "Maybe I oughta sing to him also, the way Lightning do for the calves."

Dab spat. "That'll sicken him sorry quick."

It was all I could do to hold in the urge to punch my smarty-mouth brother, one good whack, to drain the grin off his face. But instead I just watched Dabney rubbing the lead rope around the pony's neck, almost like he was scratching him with it. As I eased myself back along his flank, the pony whipped his tail, and it caught me full across the face. It made my brother laugh fit to busting. Dab sure could be an ornery cuss.

"Okay," said Dab, "we'll setcha up topside." Kneeling down, Dabney let me use his knee for a booster, so I could swing my right leg up and then climb aboard. "Next time ya mount him," Dab said, "use your left hand to purchase a solid grab to the tail of his mane. Right here. But before you kick a leg up, give his mane a gentle yank, just to alert him to what you're fixing to do."

"Okay," I said. My brother sometimes made sense.

"Pat his neck," said Dab.

I did it very gently, and Dabney shook his head at me. "Harder," he ordered. "Like this. Make a sound when ya pat his neck. That way, he'll *hear* your loving as well as feel it. It's touch, Harry. You'll touch him with knee pressure, a firm hand, and a soft voice. Touch an animal welcoming, and he's yours forever."

"Ya know," he told me in a quiet way, "it weren't too easy for Mama to dig up the scratch to purchase this here luxury animal."

I knew Dab was saying the truth. I couldn't ever remember having something just for fun that wasn't ranch-made. Every bit of money we had went to pay wages and to Cheater and Hoolie and the Otookee Bank.

"Do you think Mama shouldn't have done it?" I asked Dab.

"Reckon it was a pleasure that she couldn't resist," Dab said.

"I'm glad," I told Dabney as I leaned forward on my pony's mane so's I could stretch both arms down to hug his neck and inhale his warm pony smell.

"Yeah," he said. "So am I."

"You didn't get no pony when you were little like me, did ya?"

As he coiled the lead rope Dabney shook his head. "Nope. But I'm still glad to see you aboard yours." He took in a breath. "Providing."

"Providing what?"

"Well, providing you tend to him proper. Brush him, so his coat'll shine. Check him over every day, the same way I do for our work horses. See that there ain't no pricky old burdocks nested into his tail. And spray his underside with the Flit can that's in the barn."

"Is that all?"

Dab nodded. "It'll do for a starter."

Hugging my pony's neck, with my right cheek resting on the coarse hair of his mane, I looked at my brother. Somehow he appeared to be taller. And his face more serious than usual. Dab wasn't a kid anymore. Trouble is, I was thinking, Dabney Beecher was turning from a bossy brother into an even bossier man.

My pony nickered at Socky.

"Hang on," Dab ordered me, "and we'll stroll over and pay Socky a visit." His hand gave the rope a soft tug. "Come on, pony." Then he looked square at me. "By the way, Harry, you thought up a name for this rascal?"

"Well," I said, trying to hold in a giggle that itched my insides, "how about a name like Trudy Sue?"

Dab glowered at me as I mentioned the name of his girl friend.

It would have to be a righteous special name, I was thinking, like maybe after somebody in the Bible. Adam? Samson? Moses? Joseph? Abraham? None of the Holy Bible names that my brain was recalling seemed to fit. Looking out across Spanish Hoof as I rode my pony, I felt glad we lived here. And this meadow would offer a happy home for my new animal. Sort of like a green outdoor kingdom for a noble prince.

That was it!

"Noble," I said.

Turning around, Dab squinted at me. "Huh?"

"That's his name."

"What is?"

"Noble."

Dabney grinned. "I've heard worse."

"And now that Noble's friendly to me and all, I want to ride him alone."

Dab looked at me for a while. "Harry, you're a *limit*. I don't guess I ever met nobody near as impatient as you. But I'll tell ya what we'll do."

"What?"

"We'll *trot* Noble around in a circle, seeing that merely *walkin'* him is become so blessed boring."

"I wanna gallop, the way you do on Socky."

Dab smirked. "Sure. And then tumble yourself off, bust your neck, or maybe separate a few teeth."

"Okay, we'll trot."

I watched as Dab let out near to all of the lead rope. Then I laced my fingers into Noble's mane to get a firm purchase.

"Kick him, Harry."

My heels touched Noble's ribs. Nothing happened.

"Harder."

The second kick urged Noble forward into a slow walk, but the third touch of heels broke him to a trot. Dab stood in the exact center of the circle, holding the rope, while Noble and I trotted around and around. Waving his cowboy hat, Dabney convinced Noble to trot even faster. The trot bumps were starting to whack my bottom, but that wasn't the worst of it. My throat could taste the chicken and gravy that Poker had cooked for tonight's supper. It kept coming up higher and higher.

"Whoa," I said.

"Feel like a rest spell?"

"Yes. Yes!"

"Pull back on his mane. He'll quit. Noble probable figures that the pair of ya have spanked each other most to death."

Noble slowly eased his trot down to a walk and then stopped. I didn't wait. Kicking up my left leg, I slid off his back.

Dab scowled. "Wrong. Ya mount left and dismount on the same side. Never on the right side."

"Know-it-all."

"It beats not knowin' nothing."

Socky nickered.

As I rubbed my sore bottom I looked south across Spanish Hoof to see a sorrel horse, with a white mane and tail, cantering our way. The girl who rode the horse had sorrel hair too. I ran to greet her.

"Trudy Sue!" I was hollering.

Trudy Sue Ellsworth pulled her mare, Goldie, to a stop, kicked off, and presented me with a giant hug. She wore a soft red-and-white polka-dot shirt and jeans.

"I got me a pony."

"So I hear," she said. "I've come to admire him."

Taking her hand, I yanked toward where Dab and Noble stood waiting.

"Howdy," said Dab.

"Hi."

"His name's Noble," I said. "Do you think that fits him proper for a name?"

Trudy Sue, leading Goldie by a rein, nodded. "I sure enough *do*. Why, I couldn't have thought up a name any prouder than Noble if I'd taken all year. Isn't he beautiful, Dab?" she asked him.

"Yup." But as he answered, he weren't looking much at my pony. "He's that."

"Harry Beecher," she told me, "I'd say that *you* are about the luckiest little gal in all of Florida." She raised a hand to her chin as though studying the matter. "And maybe even most parts of Georgia."

She tickled me to a giggle. It made me feel that I'd got built out of bubbles. And I didn't know whether to hug Trudy Sue or hug Noble. At that moment I might have even hugged my brother.

"How'd ya learn I got my pony?"

"Well, Daddy saw Mr. McCabe. So he heard all the exciting news."

I watched Trudy Sue patting Noble. Her hands looked real clean and soft, like she washed an ample lot, not at all like my mother's. Hers were harder than the talons on a buzzard.

"My," she said, "he is sweet. And I can only think of one thing that's any sweeter."

"Is that Dab?" I asked.

Dabney sighed. As he looked at Trudy Sue he stood on one boot, shining the gritty toe of the other on the back lower leg of his jeans. Then he performed the same service for his other boot. To watch him made me chuckle. In his way, I figured, he was trying to slick up for appearances.

She laughed. "Lordy, no. He's not sweet at all. Leastwise, not near as sweet as you and Noble." Trudy Sue walked over to Goldie, unsnapped the catch on a saddle bag, and reached inside. Then she handed me a jar of brown preserve.

"Thanks," I said. "Is it jam?"

"No, it's rhubarb conserve. From the very first harvest of rhubarb from our garden."

"What's in it?"

"Rhubarb," said Dab.

Trudy Sue gave him a push.

"Now remember," warned Trudy Sue with a finger pointing at me, "it's not *all* for you. Some of it has to be for your mother, too. And if there's a wee bit left in the bottom"—she looked quickly at my brother—"I s'pose Dabney gets a helping."

"Thanks," Dab grunted.

"Tell you what," Trudy Sue told me. "We'll carry the jar, and I'll put *you* up on your pony." Tossing the jar to Dabney, then placing her hands under my armpits, she hefted me up onto Noble's warm back.

I noticed that Dab didn't argue with Trudy Sue the way he did with every cussed thing I said.

The three of us headed toward the house. I rode Noble while my brother and Trudy Sue Ellsworth walked way ahead, about as far in front as the lead rope would allow. Watching, I decided that Dab's way of walking looked real ugly compared to the way his girl friend moved. Dabney sort of limped along as though his legs oughta be on a horse. Trudy Sue walked with an easy swing of her hips that could have passed for a dance. Not that her walk was showy. Just graceful. It was a movement that I'd have to practice in order to look total like Trudy Sue Ellsworth when I got older. I had to admit that Trudy Sue fitted her jeans a lot more stylish than the way I fitted Dab's old ones.

Because the sunset was turning from pink to dark purple, I knew it was near to bedtime. So I didn't argue too much when Dab suggested that maybe Noble was tired too and ought to get turned out to meadow for the night. Besides, I figured as I heard him whistle to call Socky, he'd ride with Trudy Sue back to the Ellsworth place, to see her safely home.

"Good night, Trudy Sue," I told her. "Thank you for coming over to Spanish Hoof to meet Noble. And thanks for the rhubarb too." I hugged her.

"Sleep tight, Harry," she said. "And I bet you'll dream about riding your pony."

Dab handed me the rhubarb jar. "Here," he said. "You're in charge of the preserves. Show it to Mama, okay?"

He removed the rope from Noble. The two of them rode off together, walking their horses, to make the trip last longer, I suspected.

Inside, I was laughing. Because, before Dab left, I'd took notice that his front tooth sported a hunk of carrot.

Chapter 7

I saw a light in the bunkhouse.

Underneath it was conversation; most of it I heard being handled by Poke who, when he failed to win at euchre, usual blamed it all on Lightning's arrangement of the cards.

"Play," snorted Poke.

"I can't."

"Why the heck *no*?"

"Because," said Lightning, "it's your turn."

I heard a card get slapped to the table; and then the old cook howled as, I guessed, Lightning picked it up. To listen made me chuckle. I was glad Lightning and Poke had each other to scrap at.

Entering the house, I saw Mama sitting at the kitchen table, studying her papers. They were spread out in front of her, and she squinted through her specs. She looked up. "Well, how's the pony?"

"I rode him some. And I also named him."

"Well, let me share it."

"Noble—like a handsome prince."

"That's a right fitty name," said Mama. "For certain." She tipped back in her chair to bump against the kitchen wall.

"Trudy Sue rode over on Goldie. But now, as it's close to dark, Dab's riding home with her. I guess so's her pa don't ride out searching. Why she comes to seek Dabney I'll never know."

Mama smiled. "You'll know, when your heart sprouts wings."

"This here is from Trudy Sue," I said, handing my mother the preserve jar. "For all of us. It's rhubarb conserve."

Mama smiled. "I hope you thanked her."

"Sure enough did."

"She's such an angel of a girl. Inside and out."

"When I'm full growed," I said, "I certain do hope I'll favor Trudy Sue Ellsworth."

Mama nodded. "Perhaps you will."

"Not until I master a walk like *hers.*"

Mama watched while I strutted myself a turn around our kitchen, trying to parade as if my behind had a tail and I was switching flies.

Mama laughed. "Harry, you're a limit."

I stopped parading. "That's what Dab usual says. Mostly he comes out with it whenever Trudy shows up."

Mama's pencil tapped the table. "Harry, maybe it's best that whenever Trudy Sue appears, you sort of disappear—and don't tag along behind. Or shadow."

"How come?"

"Dab works our ranch all day. He's up early, when you're still abed. So when the day's over, he oughta enjoy an evening with Trudy Sue."

With a sigh I planted myself down into one of the chairs around the table to look at all the papers. "These are calf records," I said. "Aren't they?"

Mama nodded.

"All those numbers," I said. "I don't guess I savvy even a mite of it. How can ya understand all that stuff?"

Slipping off her specs, Mama rubbed her eyes. "Sometimes I ample ponder it myself." Her voice sounded thin and gray.

I fingered a paper. "What's this page?"

"This is Cow 38. This left-hand column is a history of her brood years, one line across for each of her calves."

"Where's this year?"

Mama pointed to 1933. "Right here. But let's study her last year's record. See?"

"Yup. What's the G for?"

"Sired by Gertrude." Mama's fingertip snaked along her chart. "Calf number 209. Born on March 4. Weaning weight was 412. His yearling weight was 557. And when we sold him he weighed 981."

"All I weigh is 72," I said. "Yesterday I stepped on our scales and Dabney fussed forever with those little black balancers."

"Good," said Mama. "Means you're growing like a calf." She pulled a wisp of barn straw out of my hair. "I'd be pleasured when you're Miss Harriet Beecher, growed up and tall."

I shuddered. "Can't I keep to being Harry?"

"Yes, you can. Until some handsome devil of a boy rides here to Spanish Hoof, kicks off his horse, and says, 'Harriet, you're prettier than a gob of bee honey on a hot biscuit.' "

"Is *that* what he'll say?"

"That's what your daddy told *me.*"

"Do you guess Dab says that to Trudy Sue?"

Mama wiped the lenses of her specs on the tail of her work shirt. "I don't guess it's much of our business, yours or mine, what Dabney tells his sweetheart."

"Far as I can notice," I said, "Dab don't jaw much at all to her. His talk sort of limps like a spavin horse. His eyes roll around inside his head worse'n fever. Trudy Sue cooks up all the chatter."

Mama chuckled. "With you two gals around, I don't guess poor ol' Dab gets much of a gap to even sneeze."

"He talks to Socky."

Mama eased her chair back to the table, thumping its front legs to the floor planks. "It's often easier for a boy to talk to his horse. Just the way you'll be conversating with Noble."

"I'm real happy on my new pony. Thanks a whole lot. I bet we couldn't honest afford the price you paid to Cheater. How much did Noble cost?"

———

Mama touched my face. "Not near enough, especially for somebody as sweet as you."

"I don't get it."

"Oh, you will in time. Someday—"

"That's a good far off. I'll *never* grow up. Trudy Sue looks more woman-growed every time I see her."

Mama looked at me as if she had something to say.

"Harry, let's take a walk."

"What for?"

She stood up. "My legs are cramped. And I've fussed and fretted over calfing records ample enough for one evening. Besides, there's an item out back you oughta look to."

We went out the kitchen door. I walked beside Mama toward the hen coop. The moon was halfway into a cloud.

"See," said Mama, "there's a bud on our rose bush."

I touched it. "Still green," I said, squinting. "Can't yet notice any pink to it."

"That's how it be with buds and children. They all open in their own sweet time. It'd be fooly to wish for sooner. Life fritters away quicker than early."

Mama leaned on a fence post. Resting a boot on the bottom rail, she laid her hands on the upper butt of the post to make a nest for her chin. She looked to the west, over to the final whisper of sundown.

48

"You tired, Mama?"

"Bone through. Living's hard, but quittin' is a whole bit harder. So we work our lives like we work a ranch—a day to a time."

"I s'pose," I told her.

"Every day's a little hunk of life, all its ownsome. That's why, each day ya live, there ought to be a new pony. Or a new rose."

"Makes reason to me," I said.

"Funny, but here I'm standing, on Florida sand that I own a few grains of, and the Otookee Bank owns most of. My back hurts, and my hands still burn from branding, yet we swallowed the dust of a good day's labor. And we got a rose to look up at us, as if to nod that we done it proud."

I yawned.

Mama saw me do it. "You helped your brother more'n a smart today. I knowed your thoughts were on the pony and to go pleasure with him. Thank you, Harry."

"It's my ranch too. I love Spanish Hoof."

"Good. It's home. You and Dabney got born here. And I want to die here. All we gotta do is hang on year to year. Right now our future's dangling on a calf crop. If our luck holds, it looks hopeful, Harry."

Mama rested an arm to my shoulder so that I'd lean closer to her. It felt gentle. It was a feeling I sort of had a hanker to save.

"Do you save stuff, Mama?"

She smiled. "Lots. A whole heart full. And a big trunk full, too. Trinkets and treasures."

"I bet you saved plenty in that old trunk that stands at the foot of your bed."

Mama nodded. "It be there. Some of the saving's too precious to peek at often. Only at special times."

"Like what?"

"Oh, a photograph of Clarence and me. It's turning yellow. Besides that, there's your first baby shoes. Dab's too. Plus my favorite dress, with little lavender flowers all over it. Violets, dainty and small."

As I scratched a bug bite I asked Mama how come I'd never seen her wearing her favorite dress. Not even to Sunday church.

Mama shrugged. "Oh, I'll wear it someday."

"For what?"

"When Dab gits wedded. For your wedding too, I hope. After that, only one more time."

Chapter 8

I opened my eyes to morning.

Even though it was still almost nighttime dark, I could hear Dabney in the kitchen, shaking grates in our cooking stove.

Dab was always first in his boots. Also, he was usual last to bed. He just never seemed to need ample more than a blink of sleep.

As I crawled out of bed the kitchen door banged. Looking out of my tiny window, I saw Dab trotting out through the gray shadows of mist, headed toward the bunkhouse. He carried a cook fork and a skillet.

"Poke! Lightning! I got great news for ya, boys. A circus just come to Spanish Hoof, on its way into Otookee."

I grinned, knowing that it was one more of Dab's usual tricks, the ones he'd use to shake life into our ranch hands.

Whang! Bang!

Dab was ringing the frypan louder than his big mouth. From the hen coop, the chickens even turned a bit fussy; maybe wondering how Dabney Beecher could best them in a race to morning.

"Yessir, boys," Dab was yelling. "It's a traveling circus. And all those fancy ladies are outside, doing a hootchee dance in nothing except their skimpy pink tights."

Whang! Bang! Clang!

"Dang it!" I heard Poker swear. "Lightning, ya done hid my socks again, you young devil."

"Up and at," Dab hollered. "Because the prettiest of them ladies is riding Harry's pony across the meadow. And she's jaybird *naked.*"

"Well," I heard Poker say, "if it's marriage she's got in mind, tell 'er I'm still asleep."

I saw the old man's uncombed head stabbing out through the open door. It sure was a merry sight. Especially when Lightning crept up behind him and covered his searching eyes with a dirty sock. Dabney was right, I thought. We sure had us a circus at Spanish Hoof.

"Good morning, Ruthie."

Now Dab was talking to our one and only milk cow, Ruthie, who was waiting at the bars of our shed, like usual. I heard him slide the bars to let her inside. Pulling on my jeans, I ran out of the house to collect eggs and scatter corn to the hens. Morning was starting to spook away the mist, so I could look across the graze meadow and locate Noble. There he was. I wanted to run to him and hug him hello; but I didn't tarry as there was ample to do first. As I entered the shed I could hear the click of the stanchion bars as Dabney fastened Ruthie's neck so she wouldn't shy during her milking.

I grabbed a rag. "I'll wipe off her udder," I told Dab. That was a ritual that Mama said never to skimp over. Because it just wasn't proper to milk dirty. If'n we did, too much besides milk got dusted down into the pail.

"Good gal," Dabney said.

"Me?"

He grinned. "No, I was talking to Ruthie."

I threw the rag at him. "Let me try a hand at milking again. Maybe I'm big enough now. Okay?"

Dab sighed. "Sure."

As he said it I could tell that his stomach wasn't too anxious to wait up for breakfast. Even so, Dab planted the stool under me and fetched the silver pail.

"Give it a lick," he said.

My fingers took a purchase on the two nearest teats and squeezed. Above my thumbs, Ruthie's bag was pinky full, and I could feel her Holstein warmth against my face, a big black-and-white pillow of fresh morning. I rubbed her with my head.

"That's it, Harry. Take all day."

Yanking, I produced a few white squirts. As I did it, from the corner of my right eye I saw Ruthie turn to wonder at me, the way that only an impatient cow can look at a milker whose hands don't pump fast enough.

I stopped.

"Resting?" Dab nagged me.

"Nope. I'm just adjusting higher for a tighter grip, that's all. Here goes."

Two more dribbles dotted the bottom of the pail as Ruthie let out a bored *moo*. But I wasn't fixing to quit. My fingers kept at it until Dab couldn't abide to watch; he knelt beside me, circling his hands around mine.

"Here," he said, "we'll add a mite more squeeze and some rhythm. It's like fiddle music, Harry. There's a beat to it. Sort of the way ya might tap your toe when ol' Poker whistles his harmonica."

Strings of milk, one, then another, began to ring the pail like chimes. It tinkled a real pleasing sound, and I thought I saw Ruthie nod her head.

"It's right easy once ya git your hands a firm purchase," I told Dab. "This is the best I ever yet done."

White bubbles built a dome over the milk as Dabney and I worked her teats. Left, right, left, right.

"Nothing to it," said Dab. He removed his hands and let me play solo again; the strings of milk shortened up. Ruthie gave us another *moo*. "Keep pumping, Harry."

"My fingers are getting tired."

"On a ranch ya don't measure tired, Harry. Ya measure *done*. The time to quit ain't when *you're* finished. It's when the *job* is."

"Know-it-all."

Dab's fingers closed over mine again, welcoming more milk. We really made it pour plentiful.

"No," he told me, "I don't know it all. What we tackle is whatever job orders a doing."

"Is that so," I said.

"Yup. Ruthie here is a part of it, Mama says. The trouble is, sometimes we hatch up more chores on Spanish Hoof than we can manage."

Listening to the squirts of milk, I was thinking about what Dabney had just told me. His voice, next to my ear, sounded a mite deeper than I'd heard earlier.

"How come you're telling me all this stuff?"

"Because we both gotta grow up. We're getting older. And so is Mama, in case you failed to take a notice. Ranch work's busted her apart and then stomped on all the pieces."

"Maybe if I learn to milk real quick, I'll do a little ranching myself someday, just like Mama."

I felt Dabney shaking his head. "I hope not, Harry. Besides, there ain't no such thing as a little ranching. There's a doggone *lot* of it. Ranching is hard on folks. Even on a speck of land the size of Spanish Hoof. Mama wades into it because I don't guess she knows else to work at."

It made sense to me. Papa died a long while ago. He drowned in a fishing lake before I got born. And Mama had a firm mind to make a go of it, even without him.

Dab's fingers tightened on mine as we milked, as

though he could near to read my thinking. "It's too late to save Mama from all the dirty sweat and cow dust and bank dealing."

I asked him what he meant about the bank.

"Forget it. Now, watch how we strip-milk Ruthie's faucets here, to empty her bag proper. Won't leave hardly a drop to her. Not much milk this morning. Ruthie'll turn dry unless we freshen her. Let's go eat."

We turned Ruthie out of the shed, to meadow, and then I helped Dab tote the heavy milk pail. The thin metal half-ring handle sort of bit my hand.

But I didn't gripe about it.

Chapter 9

"Noble," I said, "go a mite faster."

I'd finished all my morning chores, and the two of us were off to the north end of Spanish Hoof, so far that I could no longer see the house or the barn. All I could spot was the big wheel on top of our windmill tower. And its tail paddle.

I urged Noble another nudge, using both my heels. Yet he sure wasn't fixing to go a hoof farther.

"Okay," I said, tugging at the left side of his mane, "we'll turn around and stray ourselfs home, seeing as you're so balky."

Noble turned and walked easy. My three weeks of riding him made me feel more confident.

"Trot," I ordered him.

No dice. My pony only walked; real careful, as if to safe sure I wouldn't tumble off. Maybe, I was thinking, my pony was somehow related to Lightning. To hurry along just wasn't his fashion.

"You sure can be a cusser," I told him. "I've tended you for near to three weeks and haven't seen you hustle even once."

He didn't answer, or hurry. All he did was whip

57

his head around to snap at a bee. I hugged him, letting my neck rest forward to his mane.

"You win. We'll just walk."

I couldn't quite figure out Noble. Seems like whenever I wanted to wander off, away from the ranch, my pony would go just so far and then he'd quit.

"Mama and Dabney let me ride alone," I said, "which means I'm in charge, Noble. You best go where I say. Hear?"

If'n he heard, he sure didn't allow it to bother him even a lick. It'd be right nice, I was thinking as I rode my pony, to be the oldest person on Spanish Hoof, instead of always having to be the youngest. When you're a mere eleven, like me, everybody and his uncle tells you what to do. And then *how*.

"That's why," I told Noble, "I sort of have to be your boss. On account I sure do ache to stand, just once, at the tall end of the bossing."

Noble stopped, sniffed at a thistle bloom, then plodded on; as if to mention that he had a pony yearning of his own.

I patted his warm neck.

"I sure hope you like living here on Spanish Hoof," I told him. "You certain ought. Because it's the grandest place in the whole world to abide at. I wouldn't want to bed myself down nowheres else. Not even up on a star."

Noble tossed his handsome head.

Reaching up, I plucked a low-hanging leaf off a laurel oak and chewed it some. As I heard my belly complain I knew I was getting hungry for a noon meal that was a mite bigger than a finger-sized leaf.

"I wonder what old Poker's cooking. Probably stew, because the pot sure had more'n a swallow left over at supper last night."

Noble snorted.

Ahead I saw our Spanish Hoof buildings getting closer. My hand guided Noble some, just to make certain we stayed to the north tract of Spanish Hoof and not venture over to where Gertrude usual grazed. Our bull was too burly to mess around, Mama said. Lightning and Dab didn't dare trespass too neighborly to old Gertrude, unless they was forked on horses.

That was when I spotted the automobile.

The car was painted a shiny black and looked to me like one of the Fords we'd see on Sunday when we'd wagon into Otookee to attend church. There were two men inside it. All else I could notice was that each man was wearing a black suit.

The driver waved to Noble and me, and I waved back, even though I certain didn't know the two strange men.

"Come on, Noble," I said to my pony. "Looks like they're going to our house. Maybe those two gents are feed salesmen."

At the barn I slipped off Noble's back, watching the two men leave the Ford and walk toward our front door. My mother came to greet them, and one of the men took off his straw hat to her. The other man didn't.

Dabney and Lightning, I knew, weren't close around. Both had earlier gone to the west grazing to check out the calves and brood cows.

Hitching up Noble to a rail in shade, I started a run toward the house, to learn who our company was. But then Poker stopped me.

"Whoa," he said.

He'd come out the kitchen door on his gimpy leg, wearing a sour-looking face. The front of his apron was soaking wet, the way it usual was when he was doing the washing.

"I wanna go see who it is."

"Well, hold back a while. Your ma's probable got business inside with them birds." Poke said it like he was growling. As he looked at the house he took in a deep breath of air, then let it all out again.

"Who are they, Poker?"

Poke snorted. "Bankers." It sounded sort of like a dirty word he'd use to cuss the cookstove. "Lawyers, judges, and bankers," Poker said. "Geezers like them all look alike to me. They don't care a hooter about folks like Miz Beecher, folks who sweat in cow dirt."

"What do they want?"

Poker gave one of my pigtails a gentle tug. "I dunno. Maybe it's sort of a social call." Yet I could tell by his scratchy old voice that he wasn't perhaps telling me all he suspected.

"Maybe I'll go see."

"Hold your horses." His hands grabbed my shoulder to keep me close. "Maybe your ma wants a speck of privacy."

Poker's mouth was set grim tight, like he was fixing to say more but was holding it all in. I looked over at the house, listening, yet not hearing any of the indoor conversating.

Poker spat. "Dang them people. Office folks never seem to realize that ranchers got seven-day work to do. Let 'em in the front door an' they'll peck ya to death like a flock of buzzards."

"Did they come to peck at Mama because we owe money?"

"Likely so. Everybody owes money these days." Poker glanced over at the black Ford and spat again, in its direction. But we was standing too far away to do damage.

Then I saw Poker do a strange thing. Even though his hands were bone dry, he wiped them on his damp apron. As I looked up at his face I saw the old cook biting his lower lip. "Harry," he said, "ya know, I been here at Spanish Hoof for almost longer than I can recall. So long that I near about can't remember residing nowheres else."

"How long?"

"Oh, I was here years before you an' Dab got born. Fact is, I worked for your pa, Clarence Beecher, before he wed your ma." Poker took in a breath. "This'n here place is all the home I got. And I hope to die here, so I'll git buried in Spanish Hoof land."

I turned to look at him.

"Most of all," he said, "you Beechers is mine to tend to. You're all the family I need or want." Poke

61

winked at me. "Gosh, I never told *nobody* this before. Not even your ma. So sort of forget I spoke it out. Okay?"

"Sure," I said, pretending to punch him. Yet I knowed that what he'd just told me was an important secret that I couldn't never forget.

"Hey," he said to me, "let's set a spell in the shade. I got some dirty duds all soaking, back in the kitchen. So I can let the soap and water do the scrubbing all itself and save my knuckles."

While we sat on a bench near the doorway of our barn, Poker told me how things used to be, years back, when the very barn we were leaning against was brand-new built. But all the time we talked together, I noticed that both of us couldn't seem to quit eyeing the black Ford car.

"Yup," said Poker, "them was the days. I even treated myself and a lady friend to a trip to Belle Glade, away down south on Okeechobee Lake."

I was about to ask Poke how big the lake was, but then I heard voices. Three people appeared at our front door. I started to jump up from the bench, but Poker held me back. At the house, Mama was saying good-bye to the two banker gents.

Nobody was smiling.

We watched the two banker men step into their Ford, smoke the engine, and drive away.

"Harry," said Poker, "you gotta promise me not to pester your ma about them two geezers who come calling. Because it ain't none of your worry. Hear?"

"I hear."

"So you promise?"

Nodding, I was wondering if it was a promise I could keep. I looked at Mama, standing on our front veranda, watching the car drive away. Somehow I suspected that she'd go inside; instead, Mama just stood there, shading her eyes with one of her hands, squinting east across Spanish Hoof. Her other hand hung in a tight fist down by her side.

"Remember," whispered Poke, "no banking questions. Is that a deal?"

"Okay," I said, thinking about Mama's buying me Noble and the money he costed. A thought sudden hit me. And it didn't set very comforting inside my brain. "Maybe," I said, "it was a mistake to purchase Noble."

Bending over, Poker stared into my eyes. "Hush and don't talk that way. A kid on a cattle ranch has *gotta* own herself a pony." The old man poked a finger into my ribs. "But it might be proper," he said, "for you to run up yonder and give your mother a great big squeeze."

As I ran to Mama her face wore a beaten-down look, but when she saw me coming, it softened to a slight smile as she held out her arms to greet me.

"There's a lot more precious things than money," she said.

Chapter 10

That afternoon, Mama took herself a nap.

I was outside near our barn when I heard yelling. Looking out over the south meadow, from where I sat on the top rail of our shed fence, I saw a horse and rider coming faster than their dust. It was Lightning.

"Dab! Dab!" he was hollering.

My brother must've heard it too, because he come running out of the barn to look where I was pointing. I jumped down off the fence. Lightning reined in his horse, but he didn't bother to unhook his leg from the saddle. His spooky look seemed to be yelling without any words.

"What's wrong, Light?" Dab asked.

"Brood cow. One we was missing, last count. She's to drop her calf early. Got herself mud-stuck."

"Where's she at?"

Lightning wheeled his horse in half a circle and pointed. "Away yonder. She swamp wandered."

Asking no more questions, Dabney grabbed two

coils of rope, then jumped on Socky. The two of them galloped off, scattering dust into left-behind clouds.

I didn't waste a blink.

It took me a long scamper, across pasture, to locate Noble. He held himself quiet while I kicked a leg over his back. I punched both my heels to his ribs.

"Heeyup," I ordered him.

Following Dab and Lightning was no problem at all. Their horses had planted top-speed hoofprints that a blind coondog could've trailed. Noble helped; he seemed to realize where we were bound for, with his ears up and forward. Maybe my pony was itching to see the trouble too.

"We'll help out, Noble," I said, bumping along over his trot. My fingers clutched the rough hair of his mane.

I rode into the trees.

It was shadowy under all the big cypress where the earth, instead of looking tan and sandy, was now a black muck. Noble darted and twisted between the humps of low fan palms, avoiding the mean prickers on their stems. We came to the two riderless horses.

Up ahead, I heard voices.

I pulled Noble a mite slower, hauling him back with both hands. Dabney, I was certain, wouldn't want me to tag along. Not to a calfing. Certain not this deep into the wetlands, a place where everybody at Spanish Hoof had scolded about, warning me to keep clear.

"Gators don't spook me," I told Noble.

I heard a cow beller, sounding painful. She did it again; but this time Noble's hoofs were sloshing through a shallow puddle of swamp water, so the cow seemed farther off.

Noble stopped.

My heels dug his ribs again, three times, to urge him forward. In front of us, there was a fallen log, which Noble took his time hoofing over. He needed coaxing, so I clucked to him some. Dab and Lightning were yelling. I could see both of them, waving their hats and arms, even though I yet couldn't spot a cow.

"*Hyah!*" Dabney hooted.

I worked Noble closer. Whatever was going to happen, it promised to bloom exciting; so I certain weren't going to miss out watching. Nearer now, I saw Dab on the ground, seated, pulling off both his boots.

Then I spotted our cow. Her black body was heaving as she stood about knee deep beyond the pool of deeper swamp water. Mud had frosted her flank. Her head hung low as her body arched upward like a bucking horse.

Dab waded into the water.

"Take caution," Lightning warned him as he followed Dab into the deep mud, and both of them neared the cow. Dab, in front, sunk in water almost to his belt.

"We gotta rope her," Dabney said. "Then maybe we can swim her through the deep water, toward us."

"How?"

"Beats me. But here goes."

As they waded closer the big black animal lowered her head even more, like she didn't cotton to drop her calf. Her eyes bulged out a pop, almost exploding from her face.

"Lady," said Dab, "you sure picked one devil of a location for motherhood. Unless you're half cowfrog."

Lightning started to sing: "Black lady, black lady, stuck in a wet. Outa here, outa here, you gotta get."

The cow pumped her body.

"Lordy," said Dab. "She busted water."

Wet stuff shot out of her backside. Blood came too. The drops freckled the low leaves of a fan palm. Tiny red specks.

"Maybe she's hung up," Lightning said, "and can't birth."

Dabney swore. "I dassn't pester her. Not when she's straining her drop. But the calf'll drown."

"Maybe no."

Before my brother could say more, Lightning must have slipped into the water, snaking a rope behind him. All I saw was a cluster of silver bubbles. Then I saw him surface to spread a loop of rope beneath the cow's rump. Mud was covering Lightning's face.

"Murky down yonder," he said, his mouth yawning open to breathe and then to spit water.

The calf showed.

It was slow work. But the brood cow must've knowed her business. Inch by inch, she grunted it into Florida, all bleedy and kicking. The calf splashed into the swamp water, followed by more blood and birthsop. I kept myself hid, trying not to tremble.

"It's born," Lightning yelled.

"Pull," said Dab, snaking the rope around the calf.

They yanked, and the muddy loop tightened around the calf's middle. The cow twisted her head around to snap at the calf's birth cord, which looked half red and half white.

Hauling the rope didn't look too easy. There was no footing where Dab and Lightning now stood up to their armpits in the muck. Beyond them, the cow stayed in shallower water. The calf seemed to be pulling them closer to him and his big ma. The cow made a warning noise, lunging at them, hooking with her hornless head. Her front hoofs weren't idle. She struck at Dabney, knocking him backward and total into the water.

Dab come up sputtering. "Watch 'er hoofs," he told Lightning.

Again they jerked on the rope. The end of it

whipped back toward me. This time, the calf came along, kicking and bawling for his ma to save him. She certain heard. Forward she charged, into the deeper water, her large head pointing toward Lightning, who ducked away.

"Help me!" Dab yelled to Lightning. "Grab his head, so he don't swallow no water in his lungs."

Sliding off Noble's back, I raced over to help too. My feet were bare naked, and the water and mud sucked at my ankles, then at my knees. Grabbing the end of a rope, I pulled as hard as I knowed how. Dabney, Lightning, and the calf all seemed to be fighting each other or fighting the cow. Dabney held the calf's head with both arms; choking, spitting, coughing with each backward muddy inch.

Grabbing a fallen branch, Lightning did his best to shoo away the lunging cow, while Dab rassled the calf to shallower water, then to mud. His ma was still in the deep.

"I got him," Dab yelled.

"Good work," I told him.

Dabney's head whipped around to look surprised at me and give me a muddy wet stare. *"Harry?"*

Before he could cuss at me, I heard a noise that I would probable remember hearing until I turned dead. It was a *hiss!*

Lightning screamed. "Gator!"

Looking around, I couldn't see no gator. All I could see was the boiling water and our big brood cow churning up the mud and leaves with all four of her hoofs. She was now in the deepest water. Then I saw a large jagged tail and a creamy white belly and claws. The cow's face looked crazy.

"He's got 'er," Dab yelled. "Get the calf, Light."

"I got him."

Before I could even suck in one more breath, the pond of swamp water turned into a red pit of boiling death. I wanted to run, but the muck seemed to have a double grip on both my feet and all of my toes. I couldn't even scream.

Dab near about tore out all of my hair, because he hustled me away so quick. Lightning had the calf. There was no saving the cow. Even I knew that as I looked back to see the biggest gator I'd ever seen. His jaws tore at the cow's throat, and her blood gurgled out everywhere.

To watch was worse than dying.

I went to bed right following supper, which I was too sick to chew or swallow, and then I couldn't sleep. Not even with my eyes tight.

All I could see was blood.

Chapter 11

"Right now," Mama told me.

Leaning under a kerosene lamp, Mama held her mending basket in her lap as she sewed.

I stamped my foot, not very hard, on the parlor floor. Then I went over to our battery radio, which looked like a little brown hump, pretending I was about to turn it off.

"It's Saturday night," I said. But not too ornery because of the gator trouble I'd got myself into this past week.

Mama was darning a sock. I could tell it was one of mine because it still looked sorry with smudge, even after Poke had soaped it. "Yes, and I let you stay up an hour extra. And now it's nine o'clock. So don't start another program."

I turned off our radio with a jerk of my hand so that Mama would hear the click and reason how miffed I was.

"It's not fair. Dab's over at Trudy Sue's," I said. "Poke and Lightning went chasing into Otookee.

Seems like you and me oughta enjoy a smart of Saturday night, here to home."

"Tomorrow's chores and church. So you'll get your turn in Otookee too. Same as the others."

Facing my mother, I rested both fists to my hips, pressing knuckles into my nightgown. "Well, if you ask me, I bet them two birds catch a lot more sport in Otookee on a Saturday night than I do on a Sunday morning."

Mama slapped her leg. As she did it I saw hope and plunked myself down on the black horsehair loveseat.

"Harry," she said, "you're probable right."

My hand itched to reach out toward the radio again, before it got cold. Mama caught me testing the notion.

"*Good night,* Harry." She tapped her foot firmly.

"Good night," I said, wheeling away to head for the stairs.

"Don't I warrant a kiss?"

Coming close, I planted one to her cheek; but it wasn't too loving. Just so I'd let Mama know that I still felt tiffy about having to flick off the radio.

"Thank you, Harry. No hug?"

I hugged her. "Pretty soon," I told Mama, "my Saturday evenings are going to have to sprout a lot more pepper than this one. A lot more hairy fun." It was Poke's expression, not mine.

Mama squinted at my head. "On the subject of

hair," she said, "maybe you best exercise your brush a mite, before church tomorrow."

"I usual do."

"Good, because Sunday morning means Sunday best."

Walking over to our front window, I peeked out into the dark. "How soon will Dabney get home?"

Mama bit a thread and tossed me my sock. "Having had a recent look at Trudy Sue, I'd wager that Dab won't be home too sudden."

I planted myself down in our ladder-back chair, which was missing a slat. "Do you s'pect they're in love?"

Mama sighed. "I don't guess those two are more'n a inch away."

I thought about that for a breath. "The same way I love Noble?"

"Well now, it might even be a bit more savory."

Mama selected a white button for one of Dabney's shirts. Right then I yawned. My mother caught me with my mouth open and tossed her head in the direction of the upstairs.

"Git," she said, but with a smile.

Sighing, I stood up, gave Mama one more kiss, and went upstairs to jump into bed.

"Good night, Mama!" I yelled down.

"'Night, Harry," I heard her say. "And sweet dreams."

It sure didn't take me long to drift off. Nor did it

require much to wake me up again when I heard Dab singing, riding Socky home across the east meadow. I didn't even have to crack open my eyes. Dab always sang to his horse on the way back from Trudy Sue's.

I figured that the radio, and Dab's singing, would be the last music I'd hear. Yet I sure was ample wrong.

This time, I really did wake up, eyes and all; then crawled out of bed to my window. Dab was probable asleep by now, as was Mama. But I was anxious to wager that the noise I was now listening to was fixing to awaken all of Otookee. There was a pair of voices, both singing. One sang pretty, and the other one just hooted.

The moon was up. So I didn't have to strain my eyesight to see who was coming along the road, passing under our Spanish Hoof arch, heading to home. It was Poke and Lightning, on one horse and a mule. Poke didn't abide horses a whole bit, so he usual rode Golly into town.

They got close to the bunkhouse.

Thump!

I saw Poke fall himself off Golly to hit sand. Lightning giggled down at him. "That there is fall-off number nine, Poker."

"Eight," Poke snorted. "The one in town didn't count, because Golly weren't quite ready yet when I forked me aboard."

Their voices sounded a mite woozy, so I tallied that to some extra beverages they'd brought home, *inside*. Mama wouldn't go and scold. Because, as she told it, a working man's Saturday evening was strictly *his* business. And, she'd add, so was Sunday's headache.

Poke lay on the sand as Golly sniffed at him and then jerked up her head. Poker's breath had a way of doing damage to any nose.

"What a shot!" The old man whooped. Lying on his back, Poker clapped his hands. "Lightning, young fella, you certain can stroke a mean cue stick over a pool table."

"How much did we win?" Lightning asked, climbing down off his horse.

"Twenny bucks easy. Maybe more. And the look on that sharper's face." Poke chuckled. "You an' me was the best pool shooters that Nell's Place ever took in."

Lightning helped the old cook to his feet. "Yeah," he said, "we sure was sharp tonight. And luckier we din't get beat up."

"We took 'em," said Poke. "One by each, we collected their pay. Hot dang!"

I knew, from many an earlier Sunday morning complaint, that Poker wasn't the hottest pool player in the world. Or the foxiest bettor. But now, with Lightning for his partner, their Saturday nights in Otookee were turning to a fatter profit.

Mama never ordered the pair of them to keep clear of Nell's Place. But I'd heard her warn Dab about it.

Down below, in the moonlight, Lightning, who seemed to be not only fifty years younger than Poker but also in a far more sober state, pulled the saddle off his horse. Then he turned the mare and mule out through the gate, to meadow.

I leaned out to fix myself a better look. Meanwhile, Poke was busy trying to count up their winnings. "Looky all this'n loot," he yelled. "Hot gracious me!"

"We took 'em," I heard Lightning brag.

"Hush," warned Poke, finger up to his lips. "We dassn't wake up the boss lady."

"Don't tell me *hush*," said Lightning, trying to keep the cook on his feet. "You're the man who's makin' all the ruckus."

"Yup," said Poke. "We got over thirty bucks. I jus' located a tenner I didn't know we had. Yup, we cleaned their clocks, boy. Sunk every ball on Nell's table."

"I'm to sink me to bed," said Lightning. "You coming?"

"Okay. I jus' wished we'd had us a camera to take a photo of all them ornery faces."

"Not me," Lightning told him.

Chapter 12

Sunday came.

Like usual, we took our wagon, pulled by Golly, into Otookee to attend church. Earlier, when Dab, Mama, Lightning, and I were nearing ready to leave the house, Poke had announced that he was toting one heap of a hangover, from Saturday night, and was refusing to even shave. Mama had stared at him so silent that he changed his mind real sudden and came along the last minute. In a fresher face.

We rode through the June morning.

In church I sat next to Poker and got a sorry whiff as he sighed a few regrets about last night in town. His rough old hand kept wandering up to his head during a prayer, as if to keep it from tumbling off.

"Dang," he whispered. "Not never again."

The five of us always sat in the back, on the last pew, Mama in the middle between Dabney and me, to separate us. Lightning and Poke sat on the ends. People stared at us some; yet Mama said this was natural on Sunday, because it could be a day when a few folks figured they was holier than others. We weren't dressed too fancy.

During the Bible reading, I sighed.

Hearing me, Mama squeezed my knee as if to order me to manage a sharper purchase on my lung manners. After the reading, we busted into a hymn; one I liked, called "Sweet Hour of Prayer." Lightning sang the best, sort of like silver and gold. And people sure did turn around, or wiggle ears, so they could hear him warble out the words. Some even quit singing to listen up.

It made me feel ample proud, because Lightning's voice could ring out a lot prettier than any of *them* could hope to look in their gussy-up Sunday clothes.

Our preacher, the Reverend Jupiter Woodson, knew his business right proper. His sermon, he told us at the start of it, was called "Wings of Angels"— and he sure could let fly. He talked about Heaven and how nifty a place it was for your soul to go, on wings. I soaked in every word. So did Poker, especially during the prepare for Heaven part.

Mama smiled at Poke.

As for *sin,* Reverend Woodson didn't favor it much. "The saddest sin of all," he warned us, "is when a person destroys his own soul and body, swallow after swallow, filling his belly with the filthy swill of spirits." He rattled off a half-dozen other sins; ones that I don't guess Poke had managed to tiptoe around, or even dodge.

Our closing hymn was "Forgive Me, Lord."

Up until this one, Lightning had mostly carried the musical load for the Beecher pew. But now it seemed to be Poke's turn. He wasn't much of a singer. Not with a voice that could spook a crow. Yet, for four stubborn verses, Poke blasted out as though he suspected that this one appeal was his final snatch at salvation:

> "Forgive me, Lord, forgive me
> For all my evil done.
> For all the sorry pathways,
> Until my battle's won. . . ."

Poke had forgotten his specs, so his trembling hands held the hymnal that he and I were sharing at a full arm's reach, squinting at the words and half the time singing the wrong line. Yet even when he lost his place, Poke belted harder than when he dusted the parlor rug:

> "Forgive my wayward leaning,
> The darkness of my night.
> Forgive me, Lord, forgive me.
> And lead me tooooooooo . . . the light.
>
> Ahhhhhhhhhh . . . mennnnnnnnnnnn."

The last verse, or at least the tail end of it, turned into almost a solo by Poker. Our entire congregation had twisted around, as they stood, to hear him whack the words. Some of the folks were frowning. Most of them, however, seemed to be righteous pleased that a person who appeared to be a fallen sheep had somehow staggered his way back to the fold.

"They're passing the plate," Mama whispered.

This was my cue to cough up a dime. Dabney had to do it too. The plate started down at Lightning's end, to Dab, Mama, me, and finally to Poke, who fumbled for loose change. I heard his coins tumble to hit the hard wooden floor, and Mama's face looked at Poke as if she could hit the rafters. Then the worst happened. Instead of a quarter, what Poker's shaking hand deposited into the collection plate was a bottle cap. I saw Mama grit her teeth. But it was more than Dabney could take. He busted out a laugh that near to cracked the pew. So did I. The sight of that Pabst cap lying on a bed of silver in the bowl of the church plate was more than my ribs could handle.

Poke swore.

It was only one little word, but I had to admit I heard it clearly; and it certain was a genuine old standard, one that would grow flowers.

"Forgive me, Lord, forgive me," said Poker.

Well, maybe the Lord above was now forgiving Poke; but the faces that were all looking our way, with open mouths, weren't doing it too ample much.

On the way home from church poor old Poke hardly did much except to hunker down back in the wagon bin, to hang his head. He kept muttering, "Lord . . . forgive me." The more Poker suffered, the wider cracked Lightning's smile.

Our wagon rattled between the brace of tall posts that held up the SPANISH HOOF sign. I looked up as we passed beneath it. It was a good feeling to know, right now, that we were covering our very own land.

"Home," I said aloud, because it was a word I liked to say and to hear. I sure wouldn't want to live anywhere on earth except here, at our place. Or be anybody else but Harry Beecher.

I knew that Lightning and Poke weren't really-to-honest Beechers; not like Mama, Dab, or me. Yet they were as much a part of Spanish Hoof as any Beecher who lived here. Noble, too. We all belonged to each other.

Thinking a thought like this made me feel even a prayer cleaner than church. So, though I had on my starched Sunday dress, I jumped off the wagon seat to ride the last way between Poke and Lightning. I held Lightning's hand, while with the other arm I hugged old Poke. I didn't have to tell 'em the reason I did it.

It was something that maybe some church folks wouldn't ever understand.

Chapter 13

"Miz Beecher! Dab!"

It was Poker who was making all the midnight noise. That much I knew right off. The yelling woke me up to an instant sweat. Something was wrong. Staggering to my window, then looking outside, I couldn't see anything but nighttime. But then I heard my brother's bare heels thudding on the upstairs floorboards.

"Mama," he was hollering, "somebody's—"

"I heard 'em. I'm up."

As I opened the door to my room and peeked out into our upstairs hall, Mama, in her bathrobe, pushed me backward. And hard. "Stay inside, Harry."

"Miz Beecher, they got him!" Again it was Poker doing the screaming, and I sudden feared that somebody had come to Spanish Hoof in the darksome to steal away Noble.

"What's happening?" I asked Mama.

She didn't answer me. Hearing both Dab and Mama go clumping down the stairs, I disobeyed and trailed along too. Because I sure wasn't about to allow anybody to rustle off my pony.

"What's going on out there?" I heard Mama yelling out through the screen of our front door.

"I got a flashlight," Dab said. "Damn it. The batteries must be eaten up. The cussed thing don't turn on."

Poke yelped again. "Miz Beecher!" His voice came from down near the bunkhouse.

"I'll grab the shotgun," Mama told Dab. "You go back to the kitchen and locate the box of shells in the kitchen drawer."

I heard Dab running. And then, as I crept farther down the stairway, Mama, carrying our shotgun, opened the door and went outside. I followed as far as the door, squinting out through the torn screen.

"Don't let 'em git me, Poke." This time, I recognized another voice. It was Lightning's. Creeping out the front door and into the night, I saw three horses standing by the wagon road that led east toward Otookee. Their saddles were empty, and I couldn't see no riders anywhere nearby. Lightning yelled again. "Poker!"

I heard Dab complaining from the kitchen. "Where in heck did we put those gun shells?" I could hear drawers opening, then slamming shut. Running toward the bunkhouse, my bare foot stepped on a nest of sandspurs, sharp little balls of prickers that dug into my flesh and hurt worse'n fury.

I yelped.

"Stay back," Mama warned me.

When I saw the three men, bandanas over their faces, hats down, and their ropes, I knew it wasn't Noble they'd come for. It was Lightning. He was naked; hogtied by two ropes, kicking around in the dust, while a third man, wearing a black-and-white cowhide vest, was uncoiling a long leather bullwhip.

"No!" Lightning screamed. "Lemme go!"

Poke, dressed in his long grayish underwear suit, come running toward Mama. "It's them pool shooters from Nell's Place. Where's Dab? That gun loaded?"

"No," she said. Looking quickly over her shoulder in the direction of our kitchen, Mama said, "Dab's gone to get the shells."

Without a word, Poker went limping and hobbling toward the kitchen door as fast as an old man with a twisted leg could hustle. I followed him because the best thing to do now, I reasoned, was to find our shotgun shells. Once in the kitchen, where Dab had lit a lamp, the three of us searched in a panic; but somehow the shell box just wasn't available.

"Come on," Dab told us.

As he ran out the kitchen door Poker took a long bread knife. I grabbed a knife too, a small one, which Poke used for paring potatoes. By the time the three of us raced back to in front of the bunkhouse, Mama was standing useless. And the tall man in the cowhide vest was bullwhipping Lightning. His white body shined like a ghost.

He screamed after each crack of the whip. Mama was screaming too, yelling at the three men.

Poke made a lunge after a man, one of the two who were holding the ropes that bound Lightning to the top rail of the fence. But the man saw Poker coming, knocked the old cook to the ground, and kicked him.

"Stop it!" Mama was yelling, clicking the hammer of the shotgun into its empty chamber. "And git off Beecher land. Git!"

The other rope man pulled a revolver off his hip and pointed it at Dab and Mama. "Don't nobody try to do nothing dumb," he said. "Best you drop that gun, woman, and do it sudden," he snarled through his red bandana.

Mama dropped it.

Lightning quit his hollering. His body just slumped forward, hanging by ropes, his knees jacked; he appeared to be near to dying.

"That'll learn him," one of the men said.

"Now git off my property," Mama told him. "All of you scum."

As they pulled their long ropes off Lightning, he pitched forward onto the ground and lay motionless. The three mean men ran for their horses, mounted up, then rode into the night, eastward, toward Otookee. Their hoofbeats died in the darkness.

Crawling to Lightning, Poker used his knife to slice away the short bits of ropes that still lashed his wrists and arms. We went too. I didn't yet know whether Lightning was alive. His curly head was a mess of blood and ground sand. And his entire na-kedness was coated with grit and bleeding cuts.

He groaned.

Nobody said a word. We carried Lightning into the bunkhouse, covered him proper, lit a lantern, and washed him gentle clean. Mama's rag was pink from blood, even after dipping it again and again into the water bucket; and in a few places, Light-ning's bleeding kept on real persistent. It final clot-ted and quit.

"You'll need sewing," Mama said, gently fin-gering a deep cut on Lightning's shoulder.

Poker fetched a needle and clean white thread. As Mama stitched Lightning's pale flesh together I held his curly head in my lap, kissed him, and tried to brave away crying.

"It won't hurt long," I told him.

But the needle and thread pulling must've hurt near as bad as the whip. Even so, Lightning just lay there, swallowing all that hurting and holding Dab's hand on one side of his bunk, Poke's on the other. Stitch after stitch, he lay quiet, eyes closed into a wincing squint, singing the song that he'd sung when he'd helped out burying Poker's dead cat.

It was a sweet and gentle song, the kind of a slow tune we'd expect from somebody who'd proved to be so tending with our animals. As he sang it, real low, I sort of heard him crooning it to a bleeding bull calf that had just got hisself cut and branded.

Lightning had called it "Sundown."

Chapter 14

Poker sighed. "It's my fault, Miz Beecher."

The four of us still huddled around Lightning's bunk, inside a yellow circle of lantern light, the one under which our two hands usual played their evening card game, euchre. I held Lightning's fingers.

"How so?" Mama asked Poke.

"Well, the pair of us went to town, to Otookee last week, and I shouldn't have did it."

"Did what?" Dabney asked him.

"Seems I was dry for a drink. So I took Lightning into Nell's Place. We didn't intend no harm. All we was fixin' to do was maybe shoot us a cue of pool and flush our whistles with gin."

Mama looked at our cook. "Poker," she said, "seems to me that an old puncher such as you oughta salted away more smart."

Poke scratched his underwear suit, under an arm, with a slow hand. "Yeah," he said, "I certain ought."

Mama said, "There's places in Otookee where I go. And other spots I keep away clear of, and just maybe that should apply to you and Lightning as well as to the rest of the world. But it's no business of mine where you two gentlemen spend your time, or your money, on a Saturday night in Otookee. It's a free country."

"S'pose it is, Miz Beecher."

All during, Lightning didn't mutter a word. He just lay quiet on his bunk, breathing heavy, under the blanket that Dab had spread over him. It had surprised me some, earlier, to watch Mama doctor a total naked man. Yet she done it without a hitch. Maybe folks in Otookee would've called it a sin. But it couldn't be. Not the gentle way Mama tended Lightning's hurt.

"Lightning," she told him, "there's ample variety in the human nature. So don't start reasoning that our world's a sour place to rest in, 'cause it ain't. Most folks lean closer to goodness than they do toward mean. Even pool shooters."

Lightning nodded his head.

I picked up my little paring knife from where I'd dropped it onto the bunkhouse floor. "I'd like to get even," I said.

"No," Mama said. "I don't guess we'll fritter away our living or waste it on hate."

Poke shook his head. "Doggone it, Miz Beecher, I think Harry's right. Seems like we oughta chase them three buzzards and settle up."

Mama pointed a finger at Poke. "We'll get even. What's more, us folks on Spanish Hoof'll come out away ahead."

Poke scowled at her. "How so?"

I saw Mama smile. "We'll live happy, that's how. And that oughta push us a lot further ahead in life than the nightrider folks who don't do nothin' more than tote around guns, whips, and ornery. Men like that poison their own wells."

"You're right, Mama," said Dab. "They live sad."

Hearing the way Dabney said it sort of nudged me to stare at my brother. He sounded like a man instead of a boy. Even though he'd said his words in a soft voice.

Mama touched Lightning's sweaty face. "Men like the three sore losers who come tonight punish themselves ample," she said, "for their entire life long. That's the way it be with hating. It cuts a soul deeper than a whip'll do. And the scars don't never git sewed tight."

Poke nodded.

"Perhaps," said Mama, "before we final go to sleep this night, we should all lower our heads and beg the Almighty to forgive those men. Even though I'd like to give each of 'em a swift kick."

I heard Poker snort. "Well," he said, "if'n that's what you request us, Miz Beecher, I reckon I'll pray it proper."

"Yes'm," said Lightning. "Me too."

It wasn't more than a weak little whisper. Yet hearing Lightning utter it made all of our heads turn to watch, as he tried out a grin.

"On us Spanish Hoofers," said Mama, "there be a thicker hide than a lot of folks would ever hope to guess."

One by each, Mama looked at all our faces. As she did it Poke reached out to hold my hand and then squeezed it. He spoke to Mama. "Spanish Hoof's a special Heaven, Miz Beecher. I don't own this place. But it somehow do sure own me."

Lightning moaned.

Mama bathed his face again with a wet cloth. Her hands moved real careful. "I know it hurts," she said. "Cut to a pride sometimes bites deeper than cut into flesh. But I figure you're man enough to stand up to both."

"He certain is," said Poke.

Mama looked at our cook. "I sure could use a merry tune on that squawky old harmonica. Go fetch it."

Poker hunted around, overturning several of his old coffee cans of saved-up junk, until he final located it. Before raising it to his lips, he whacked it a few times on his knee, to shake loose any grit that might have nestled into the holes.

"Okay," he said. "What'll she be?"

" 'Red Wing,' " I told him.

Poker grinned. "Good selection. On account that happens to be one of my hottest." Poke sneaked into it, and the rest of us sang along, tapping our toes to the rhythm. Yet, as I sang, the words didn't come out happy. It was like we was all pretending a smile.

"Oh, the moon shines tonight on pretty Red Wing. / My heart is pining. / The moon is shining. . . ." We tried to hustle up a fair noise, and when we all final quit, old Poker was puffing for air. During the song it seemed a bit strange not to be able to listen up to Lightning. His lips had moved without giving out much music.

"Lightning," said Mama, "our sorry tonsils couldn't ever repay you for all the sweetness you've sung to our ears. Not if we was to sing halfway to next Friday."

"Right," I said.

Mama smoothed Lightning's curls with her hand. "And remember one more thing," she told him. "I'll serve as your ma any time you need me."

"I bet you're healing real good now," I told Lightning, "with all this prosperous music to spirit ya." But, saying it, I thought about how sad our singing had been.

Lightning looked at me, then at the little paring knife that I still held in my hands. I guessed he knew why I'd earlier grabbed it as the trouble was starting to brew up bad. He knew without my telling him. Reaching out a hand, Lightning gentled the knife away from me, handing it to Mama. Then he looked my way with a quiet smile, shaking his head in a very slow way, as though to tell me things that he couldn't put to words. He closed his eyes. As I pulled the blanket up under his chin I watched his smile widen.

Mama stood up, trying to shake a late cramp out of her legs. "Well," she said, "so much for shooting pool on Saturday night at dear old Nell's. And winning other men's wages."

She looked square at Poker as she said it, and I saw the old cook's face wince up. He didn't stare back. Instead, his eyes sort of fell down to inspect the gray of his underwear. Then it hit him. He looked up again, at Mama, his face wide open in shock.

"Precious be, Miz Beecher. I been performing all this time in nothin' but my underthing."

Mama yanked the belt of her bathrobe a tug tighter. "Dearie me," she said in her lofty church-social voice, pushing up her nose with the tip of a finger, "I do believe I'm fixin' to swoon away with a touch of the vapors. Seeing as," she said, turning around a complete flourishy spin, "I'm so delicate bred."

I thought Dab would split a gut. And it all certain made *me* chuckle fit to bust.

"Mama," I said, "you're a limit."

"She sure be," said Dabney. "You name any ol' pain in this world, and I bet Violet Beecher could heal it."

Mama hugged Dab and me. Then we all said a good night to Poker and whispered one to Lightning, who seemed asleep, and left the bunkhouse to Poker, who blew out the lamp.

Before we reached the house, Mama stopped, turned, and looked back at the bunkhouse. "By rights," she said, "we oughta report this outrage to Sheriff Grimmett. But there'd be little purpose in that. And probable less done about it. In a way, Poker and Lightning got what was coming to 'em."

"No," said Dab. "You don't mean that."

Mama sighed. "Not all of it. Because they took a lick more'n they deserved. But it could've worked out a whole lot worse. A woman can't order her hired hands to stay away from places like Nell's. I guess all we can do is help patch 'em up when it happens. Whether or not Poker and Lightning were cheating at the pool table, or a card table, I don't hunger to know."

Dab looked at her. "Mama," he said, "I don't guess I ever heard you speak so—so *hard* about people."

"Me neither," I told her.

She looked at each of us in turn. "Life's got a way, sometimes, of turning a woman hard. Life, dirty cows, and one or two stiff-collar bankers."

Reaching out her thin arms, she hugged Dab on one side of her and me on the other. The sleeve of her bathrobe felt comforting around my neck.

"I never been one to do much crying," she said. "Yet while I was stitching up that boy tonight, I come a lot closer than anyone could ever guess. In a way, I got my two sons, a daughter, and Poker for a pa. Guess I'm just plain lucky."

I hugged her hard. "So are we."

Chapter 15

"Hoolie's come," Poker told me.

I sat in the kitchen, listening to Poke teach me the inside secrets of spice cookery. As he stood at the sink, murdering the hide off a potato and turning it from a brown giant into a white midget, he looked out the sink window.

It made me jump down off my stool and surrender my job of shelling peas so quickly that I scattered a flock of green marbles.

"He's here to shod Noble," I said.

I dashed out through the screen door, banging it, to race down to where Hoolie Swain had rested his wagon to a whoa. He'd climbed down off the bench, moving his chubby body with all the caution that dreads hot weather. As I arrived Hoolie was already knee deep into a chat with my mother.

About every two months Hoolie Swain came to Spanish Hoof to heft up each hoof of all our horses. I sort of liked watching Hoolie ply at his trade. Mama said he was about the best blacksmith in Otookee.

"Howdy, Mr. Swain," I said.

"Hello there," he answered back. "I hear tell you got a new pony. That so?"

"Yup, certain is. I'll go fetch Noble so you can take yourself a short look. Guess ya didn't see him on the day you brung us that load of citrus pulp."

With a scoot to the barn, I grabbed a halter rope and then ran across the south meadow to where Noble stood waiting for me, under oak shade. He looked at me as though wondering what kind of a nut would run on such a swelter of a day. Golly, our mule, was also nearby. She stared a mite too, the way only a mule can look at a fooly human.

"Come on," I told Noble.

By the time we got back close to the house Mama and Mr. Swain were talking about the Depression, whatever that was. From the general drift of it, I guessed it had something to do with hard times and folks being let go from the turpentine mill.

"These days," said Hoolie to Mama, "I do ample more'n smith to keep bread on the table. One or two days a week I usual tackle a few odd jobs for Dwayne Ellsworth."

"So I hear," said Mama. "Well, let's check out the stock. You aim to shoe hot, don'tcha, Hoolie?"

Hoolie Swain mopped his sweaty face. "Sure enough do, Miz Beecher. 'Specially for you, on account you once said you don't trust a smith who'd shoe a horse cold."

Mama nodded. "A horse is like a woman," she said. "It wants to slide its hoofs into warm slippers. Chilly iron won't do a penny's good."

"Hot it be," Hoolie said. "Well, where'll we start, Miz Beecher? I don't guess if'n we spend the whole morning in gossip we'll solve the worry about hard times."

"No," said Mama, "not blessed likely."

"I reckon you could begin on my pony, if it's okay. Please?"

Mama nodded. "Okay."

Hoolie ambled over to where Noble stood, patted his pinto flank, and then bent to heft up a hoof.

"Will he need new shoes?" I asked.

Hoolie Swain chipped a flick or two of mud from Noble's hoof with his thumbnail. He held the hoof gently between his chubby knees, then looked up. "Not right yet," he said. "But he ought to git his hoofs shaved and then I'll merely reset the irons."

"Reset 'em hot," Mama told him, and left.

Hoolie grinned. "You're the boss lady." With a shrug he started his fire.

As the sun was climbing the sky I reasoned that Hoolie Swain weren't too joyful about neighboring a fire. I watched him waddle to the tailgate of his wagon, hook two beefy arms under his anvil, and then rest it atop the old tree stump where he usual tackled his work. A few other stumps were close, so I asked him why he always selected this one.

Before answering, Hoolie fetched his heavy hammer. "Here's why." Standing at his anvil, he hung his right arm straight down to extend the hammer out level. "Harry, that's how a smith sets the height of his anvil, to keep his arm straight down as he strikes a blow. Make sense?"

It made a smart of sense to me, now that he'd explained it out; so I nodded and told him so. I liked to get taught all kinds of stuff, even though I wasn't exactly dreaming about someday becoming a blacksmith. Noble snorted, as if to tell Mr. Swain and me that he was anxious to be the first customer. It caused our blacksmith to grin.

"Bring your pony," said Hoolie.

I did. Then I watched the big man patting Noble, giving his back an easy rub, and talking to him in a voice near as soft as Lightning's.

"Around animals," he told me, "ya best begin with a lick of kindness, to make friends. You agree?"

"Yup," I said. "I certain do."

"Remember this, girl. Whenever you work on a animal that could kick, ya pick up a front hoof first. Hear? Thataway, a pony'll custom to ya while you're out of harm's way."

Working real gentle, he scraped away some dirt around Noble's hoof rim and wiped the hard pulpy frog with a rag. After removing the shoe, he pared the horn shorter. He tossed me a half-circle clipping of hoof and watched me catch it.

"See how wet and near-to-soft a hoof really is?" he asked me.

I felt it, and it was just that.

"Believe it or not," he said, "there's folks in this world who never bent up a horse leg to examine what a hoof's really like. To me, hoofs favor people. No two of 'em are twins. Leastwise, I never seed two that be."

I thought about that a mite and decided that

maybe it held a smack of truth to it.

"Never purchase a hard-hoofed horse," he said. "Because, chances are, that animal'll harbor a nature that's equal steely." He made one more smooth cut around the entire edge of the hoof. As he worked, Hoolie rubbed his head on my pony's flank, to quiet him.

Inching in to cop a closer look, I asked, "How much do you know to shave off?"

Without looking up at me, Hoolie said, "Just enough to let his frog hop, to take the shock off his legs. This'n here frog is Noble's spring. It's what'll bounce his gait so's he won't drag trot. He'll step out high an' proud if his hoofs feel happy. Same way amongst people too. When your feet hurt, ya ache all over."

Hoolie burned a shoe in his fire, then clanged it on the anvil with his hammer. While the shoe was roasting, he'd asked me to fetch him a bucket of water, which I did righteous quick. As he dunked in the red iron ring, a hiss popped up to match the steam.

"There," he said. "Now that's a warm slipper."

He fitted the shoe to Noble's filed hoof, then pounded in all its nails. The sharp nail points poked up, but Hoolie twisted off each one with his tongs. All I could see was a neat row of tiny silver stars.

"Looks tidy," I told him. "But what I like best about you is the way you work so careful and gentle kind."

Hoolie Swain smiled at me with a red face. "Thank

you, Harry. A man usual appreciates it when his work's valued."

"Do *girls* ever grow up and be blacksmiths?"

He shook his head. "Not hardly. It ain't proper work for a lady to tackle. Anyhow, that's how I look to it. Millie, that was Mrs. Swain, used to be so fragile, so wispy light, that folks in Otookee used to ogle at us when we'd walk the street together, her on my arm. But I didn't pay it mind. Nary a mite, because we was so happy. Her little, and me enormous. Lord, how I do miss my lady."

"I'm sorry she died."

Hoolie wiped his face. "Yeah, me too. Some days I ponder what's the sense in keeping alive. But then I meet up with a youngster, like you, who owns herself a pony that needs shod, and I know why the Almighty sent me here."

He patted Noble with a big hand.

"Funny thing," he said softly, "but I don't never talk about my wife to people. Can't figure how come I recent done it to you. Maybe 'cause your mother talked about slippers. At home, under our bed, I still got Millie's. They're so little and pink. I keep 'em both even, and handy, foolishing myself to hoping she'll come back to me."

Hoolie didn't say much more. All he did was complete his work on Noble, plus to the rest of our horses, took his pay, thanked Mama, and left.

As I went to sleep that night my mind saw Millie's slippers, still waiting beneath the bed of Hoolie Swain.

Chapter 16

"Stand still," Mama told Dab.

"Can't," said Dabney. "I itch all over me."

My brother was standing on a chair in our kitchen, dressed up fit to star in a circus. Or a funeral. He was wearing his good blue suit, a pair of Papa's black church shoes that shined brighter than wet coal, and a necktie that was fixing to throttle his face ever redder.

Mama muttered something. But I couldn't quite catch all of it because her mouth was full of pins.

Dab looked down to where Mama, on her knees, was working away at the bottoms of each of his pantlegs. Her scissors snipped away a loose thread. One cuff was still turned up but the other was down. He sure had sprouted up tall.

"They look okay," said Dab.

"Hush," ordered Mama, her needle adding a few more stitches to the bottom hem. "You can't go proper to a dance with a good half of your socks showing."

Dab squirmed. "Nobody'll notice."

"Nobody," said Mama, "except for Trudy Sue. One look and she'll wonder if'n a flood's coming and you've already hoisted up your pants for wading."

"They won't look right without cuffs," Dabney said.

"Cuffs, my boy, aren't exactly supposed to hang halfway between your knees and your ankles. Lettin' 'em down'll add another four inches. From the measure of how you've growed, we'll necessary every blessed inch of it."

All during the conversation Poke stood over at his sink, washing up the supper pots. I guessed Poker sudden figured that he'd kept silent about Dabney's appearance long enough. So he turned around to stick in his two cents.

"Well," said Poke, "if'n ya ask me—"

Mama spat a pin at him. "I don't rightly recall asking for more opinions, seeing as I've noticed the costumes *you* deck yourself out in when you're headed for Otookee on Saturday nights."

Poke grunted, Lightning giggled, and Dab stomped one of his too-big shoes on the wooden seat of the chair he was standing on. To be helpful, I crawled over to pick up the pin and returned it to Mama.

"I'll be late," Dab whined. "They're coming to get me any minute."

"Don't fret on that matter," said Mama. "Regardless of what time it is, you can count on the fact that Trudy Sue is still at home. She'll be fussing with her hair."

Dabney asked, "How do you know?"

"Because," said Mama, "believe it or not, I was a gal once, and boys used to wait downstairs for me to gussy up to ready. That's how."

"He looks okay to me," said Poker.

Lightning grinned, as if to say that Dab appeared good enough for him as well.

"I think Dab needs a haircut," I said.

My brother shot me a "just wait'll I git ya" look, warning me to butt out of offering my opinion. But it was too late. Mama stood up, glancing upward at Dabney's hair; then she clicked her scissors as if they were anxious to perform.

"Sit," she ordered him.

"Now?"

Poke usual cut Dabney's hair. He did it only twice a year, for two special events—on the day before school, in early September, and on the Saturday prior to Easter Sunday. Twice a year seemed to handle the job. Except for right now.

Mama handed Poke her scissors. "Sit down, Dabney, and not a word about it. Hear?"

"No," said Dab. He still stood on the chair.

"Why not?"

"Because I already got my good shirt on, and the doggone hair'll fall into my collar to make me itch all night."

"You look a mite shaggy," said Poker.

"Dang it all," Dab groaned. He final did sit down in the chair. "I never figured that going to a dance would fashion into a family meeting."

"We're proud of you, that's all," Mama told him. "And I don't guess any of us cotton to havin' ya look shorter than best."

Poke grabbed Dab's longest lock and snapped at it with the scissors. Dab squinted. "It's so hot in this kitchen I'll roast dead before Trudy Sue and her pa even get here."

"Hold quiet," Poke ordered him.

As my brother was now seated, with his pants yanked up some to preserve the crease from Mama's flat iron, I noticed one more trouble.

"Dab's socks don't match," I said.

He almost kicked at me. "Darn ya, Harry, keep out of it. Okay?"

"They don't?" Mama bent over to look.

"One's blue and the other one looks sort of dark greeny," I said.

"Maybe," said Mama, "soon's Poke completes his barbering, you'll have time to dash upstairs and change."

"I oughta go *naked*," said Dab.

Lightning almost split his stitches laughing. Poke grinned as well. Even my mother was smiling at that crack. In fact, all four of us were bending grins as we huddled around the only person, our dancer, who wasn't even about to share in the fun. In a way, I was starting to feel sorry for ol' Dabney, who'd begun to sweat more than ample.

"Here," I said, "let me fix your bow tie."

"It's *fixed*," Dab snarled at me.

"But it sure looks crooked to me. Ya got one flap hanging down and, at the other end, one's sticking straight up under your chin."

"I'm not going," Dab said.

"Sit still," Poker told him. "I darn near chopped my own finger because ya fidget around so cussed much."

Dab jumped to his feet. "That's it! I'm as ready as I'll ever be. Besides, I can't even dance a step."

"Hold on now, son," said Mama, "and we'll practice one more time." Standing in front of him, she took his right hand to place around the belt of her work jeans. "Like so." She took his left hand into her right.

"My hands already know, Mama. My chief problem's what to do with my stupid feet. I sure wished I'd wore my cowboy boots instead of shoes. They feel too roomy."

"One," said Mama, "and two . . . and glide, glide, glide. See? Isn't that a ringtail cinch?"

"Dab ain't gliding," I said.

"Can't ya pack her off to bed?" Dab asked, glaring at me with narrowing eyes.

Outside, a car horn honked.

Dab near to jumped out of his blue suit. "That's

Mr. Ellsworth. And I ain't even mastered the rhythm of it yet."

All five of us raced to the front door and out on the porch to wave to Mr. Dwayne Ellsworth, who'd arrived in his Ford to haul Dab and Trudy Sue to the dancing place.

"You look handsome," Mama whispered. "Even without cuffs. Your stockings won't show as long as you never sit down."

"Or stand on a chair," I said.

Trudy Sue was sitting in the back seat of her daddy's Ford, all spruced up in a white dress with a few light blue ribbons to trim it fancy. I'd never seen her look so beautiful.

Dab stopped.

"What's wrong?" Mama asked him.

"I gotta throw up supper."

"No," said Mama. "It'll all pass. Soon's ya git there and notice your friends and how nervous *they* all be acting, your gut will settle quicker than a pregnant mare."

Dab turned to Mama. "Thanks," he said. "If'n I live through this, I reckon someday I'll be tough enough to be a genuine Beecher."

Chapter 17

"Have fun!" We all waved.

Mr. Ellsworth's black Ford turned around by our barn, rutted a circle in the sand, then sputtered off down the road, passing under the distant arch that said SPANISH HOOF on the other side. We watched it shrink out of sight.

"I sure hope they have a good ol' time," said Poker.

"They certain will," Mama said.

"Do you s'pose," I asked, "that Trudy Sue'll notice that Dabney's socks don't match?"

Mama touched my shoulder. "Even if she *does*, Trudy Sue won't never mention it, or let on, if'n she's truly a lady. And she is."

We sat on the porch swing together, just Mama and me, listening to the bugs of July choir up. As we swung gentle, forward and back, the upper chains squeaked merry to their hinges.

"You look tired, Mama." She also was looking a mite olden, but I didn't mention that.

She patted my knee. "I'm wrung out. I never

thought we'd groom him ready at the rate we was going. Yet he really did look handsome, didn't he?"

"Sort of. Trudy Sue looked a lot prettier, if ya ask me."

Mama nodded. "She's a lovely girl. What pleases me so is because she's pretty inside as well as out. Always was. And a big help to her mother, feeding all their ranch hands." My mother tilted her head back, closing her eyes. "When you grow up—ya know, Harry, I can bare wait to deck you out for your first dance."

"Honest?"

"Having a daughter, like you, is a growed woman's way of hanging tight to memories of girlhood."

"If'n I git married," I said, "I'm fixing to have all daughters. So they won't suffer having a Dabney Beecher to boss 'em around."

Mama opened her eyes to look at me. "Dab's decent to you lots of times. And you know it."

"I know. But he still hankers to order me around ample. He wouldn't let me straighten up his bow tie. And I could've fixed it to look a lot more proper than the way *he* had it tortured."

"Well," said Mama, "a boy's necktie is sort of a personal item. The way a man knots his tie has a way of sending a message to the whole world. Kind of the way you ribbon a bow in *your* hair." She sighed. "I'm glad you're not growed up yet. I need you for company." Mama let out a long breath.

"Harry, I hope you're never alone the way I am. Never."

"You're not alone."

Mama brushed back her hair. "Oh, sometimes I am, girl."

"When?"

"Usual late at night when I'm too ranched out to even work up a sleep. Too tired to snooze or snore. Those times, I just lie awake, alone in my big bed, and review all I know about Spanish Hoof, and where we're all headed."

"To where?"

"God alone can answer that. Perhaps that's what comfort there be in the future. Nary a soul of us knows what's awaiting down the road."

Listening to Mama, I looked down to discover a rip in my shirt. "I best mend it up," I said.

"You best do." Mama smiled at me.

"Maybe," I said, "it's near time I took over all the mending chores."

"That's decent of ya, Harry. And thank you."

"You and Dabney work harder on Spanish Hoof than Noble or I do. So maybe I oughta chore at more stuff to earn my keep. Sort of like Poke and Lightning."

Right after I'd said all that, I heard a happy holler from the bunkhouse. Then a distant cuss word.

"Euchre," said Mama. "Those boys certain do enjoy their card playing. If arguing half a night is any sign."

"Ya know," I told Mama, "when Dab was all gussied up for the dance party, both Lightning and Poke looked at him prouder than pie."

Mama smiled. "Indeed so. Like they wanted to haul him into Otookee and learn him to shoot pool at Nell's Place. Them rascals."

"I hope if Lightning goes there again, he don't win no money, like the last time."

"Me too, child. We can be grateful he healed so quick. Inside too. When ya stroll into a panther's cave, ya can't wonder at gittin' clawed."

"Mama, if I was a growed lady, married to Lightning, I'd order him never to go there again. That's what *I'd* do. I'd tell him to choose between holding me or a pool stick."

Mama chuckled. "Harry Beecher, you're a limit. And a lot more besides. I see the lady in ya blossoming out, day upon day." Mama closed her eyes again. "Someday, sooner than I can probable handle, you'll be full-out matured. Too big to ride Noble. And away too growed only to be my daughter, or Dab's baby sister."

"What'll I be?"

"Oh, you'll be Miss Harriet Beecher. For a spell. And you'll be going to dances in a white gown, wearing flowers. That's just the surface of it. Inside, you'll be a mix of guts and tenderness, and that's our blessed blend of being human."

"I'm gonna have babies too. Lots of little girls."

"All daughters?"

"Yup. Well, maybe *one* boy, just so's we'll have

ourselfs somebody to handle a lick or two of the heavy work, like Dab does."

"Dab's a sweetheart. Oh, he's an awkward pup at dressing. Probable at dancing too. Yet he's a man almost. Sweats like a man do. But he's no more determined than my daughter. You're strong, Harriet. I feel it when we're alone together. You've pecked up a lot of Spanish Hoof grit in your craw. So much of it that it'll oft startle me."

"I wish I had me a sister."

"If," said Mama, "our friend Trudy Sue comes to live here, someday, at Spanish Hoof, I expect you to treat *her* like a sister. With respect. I don't want the brace of you women to bicker away at each other's throats like two old hens."

"Trudy Sue—*here?*"

"Yes, it's quite possible. And soon. She'll be Dab's wife, Harry. I've figured that for years."

"Well," I said, "if that's how you reason it, then it must be so."

Mama smiled. "I hope so."

"How soon'll Dab git hitched up?"

She shook a finger at me. "That," she said, "ain't for a mother or a sister to decide. God decides that. Sooner or later, Dabney'll stretch up to full growth. Not in height, in manhood. And he'll know the harvest of a home."

I liked the way Mama said things. Her words sort of grew up from solid ground, like garden greens.

It was a quiet night, except for a once-in-a-while

---

holler from the euchre game. Whenever the wind blew from the south, like tonight, we could hear the bugs and whippoorwills from the swamp. Remembering the gator still gave me the shivering allovers.

Mama looked at me. "You cold?"

"Nope. I was just thinking some on what happened, at the swamp. That big ol' gator might've got Noble instead of a cow."

My mother sighed. "That isn't exactly why I tanned your seater. It weren't because you put *Noble* in harm's way."

"I put me."

"Yes!" Mama squeezed my knee with her hard fingers. I flinched. "And never again, Harry. Before you volunteer to help out, and thanks for doing it, you first ask if you can tag along. Hear?"

"I hear. Well, at least we got ourselfs a new calf. I bottle-fed him again today. Maybe soon, if what Dabney says is straight, we can match him up to a cow that lost her own. That is, if'n the two will take to each other. Anyhows, we got Spanish Hoof a new calf."

Mama shook her head. "Not exactly, girl. What it actual boils down to is this. The Otookee Bank got a new calf. And our sweat to raise it."

I hugged myself, for warmth. "I don't care a sneeze about some old bank. Spanish Hoof's ours, not theirs. We work it. So it be *our* land."

My mother bit her lip, chewed on it, and then

caught me watching her. She quit. Yet her mouth stayed in its tight line.

"Ours," she said softly. "Yours someday. It'll fall to you and Dabney, equal shares. I s'pect folks in Otookee might squint at our house and snicker, because it don't stand so uppity fancy. Yet there's not one single place in town I'd trade even for. Nary a one. I just pray the bank people don't tighten on me, or turn mean if we miss a payment. We won't miss often if the calves all fatten and prosper. The bankers know that at least."

"Are they mean as a gator?"

Mama stood up to stretch. She walked back and forth, looking up at the summer moon, and sighed. "Gators ain't mean, child. All of God's critters fill a purpose, a plan. Gators—and bankers."

"And us ranchers."

I stood up proud to say it. Mama came to me to hold me closer than I'd ever felt before. Her body felt so hard that I was afeared she might snap.

When we sat in the swing again, I wanted to ask Mama to explain to me more about our calves and the Otookee Bank people. Yet I held quiet because I'd promised Poke. Besides, my eyes were sagging, then they closed. Even though I could hear the tiny whine of the chain loops above us as our swing swung back and forth, I was near to dreaming about Noble. And hoping he was asleep out in the meadow, dreaming about me.

Mama said something about bedtime, but I don't

guess I heard it all. The next thing I was aware of was car lights flashing in my eyes, some laughing, and an engine running.

"Dabney's home," Mama told me.

She took herself up from the swing seat. I went too, rubbing both my eyes. Just about everybody seemed to be talking, laughing, and thanking. I remembered that Trudy Sue got out of the car with Dab and hugged me a good night. She smelled pretty as summer.

As the Ellsworths' car drove away I felt Dab picking me up in his arms, carrying me inside the house.

"Well," asked Mama, "how was the dance?"

"Great."

"Did ya stomp on Trudy Sue's feet?" I asked.

"Nope," said Dab as he carried me up the stairs. "But I sure stomped on everybody else's."

Chapter 18

July melted us to August.

We got our milk cow, Ruthie, bred to a Holstein bull over to Mr. Ellsworth's place. I wasn't allowed to watch, and it made me madder than spit. Dabney said she'd drop a calf come spring, and that was how she would keep producing table milk. Also for the orphan calf.

But the really good part was the fact that I'd get to raise up Ruthie's calf, whenever it came. Just me alone.

"Ruthie," I said, one misty morning right after Dab and I had milked her, "when your mothering time comes, please don't wander off to the swamp. Hear?"

Whether she heard or not, Ruthie flicked her ear at a deer fly, the kind that bite meaner, according to Poker, than cheap whiskey cuts a gullet.

I shot the fence bars to turn Ruthie out into the meadow to graze, then I walked a ways with her. Mama wouldn't yell at me for doing so, because Ruthie was the only cow I was allowed to go near.

Our main herd of Black Angus, according to what Mama told me, was an entire different breed of animal. They was beef. Not used to the touch of a human's hand, so I best back off and let 'em be.

Ruthie didn't act very neighborly with our Black Angus, I was thinking. She kept pretty much to herself and her own grass. Noble was the only animal she'd tolerate as a nearby grazer.

Our beefs stayed away. They munched on grass alongside a flock of white egret birds, with long bills and longer legs, that nestled up close to eat cattle ticks.

"Noble," I called.

He came trotting to me through the lifting clouds of morning mist, as if he'd sudden been born out of a dream. He sure knew, I thought, that the two of us belonged to each other. His nose butted my chin, real gentle, just before he let me present him a big warm squeeze.

"Good morning, Noble."

Holding still, he allowed me to vault up on his dewy back, standing real quiet until he figured I was seated and safe settled. Then he walked.

"Hey!" I said. "What's over yonder?"

Using knee pressure, plus a gentle tug to his mane, I turned Noble to the east, toward Otookee, because I saw a dark shadow of a shape lying under one of our spreading live oaks.

Riding closer, I saw it was a calf. No cow was near him. He just lay there, appearing to be asleep; like he didn't cotton too much to morning and another hot Florida day of grazing his weight gain.

Taking caution, I slipped down off Noble's back to tiptoe close. It was plain to see that the black calf wasn't asleep. His eyes were awide open. But he didn't look too regular normal. Not to me. The calf's glassy eyes were milky white and, I then saw, crawling with red fire ants.

"He's dead, Noble."

The calf looked fat to me. His legs were swollen and his belly all puffed up worse'n a party balloon. Somebody, or something, had certain done him in.

Jumping on Noble, I kicked him in the direction of our house. My pony really could let out a gallop whenever he was mooded to. Like right now.

"Dab! Mama!"

I ran into the kitchen, where they were still slurping their breakfast coffee. Mama, Dab, and Lightning sat at our round kitchen table. Poke was kicking the stove and apologizing to the world in general about the quality of his bacon and scrambled eggs. The old cook stared at me.

"What's wrong, Harry?"

"Plenty," I said. "A calf's down."

"Where?" Mama asked me.

"Over east. I was aboard Noble, and we spotted him sprawly under an oak, colder'n dead."

Poker stayed behind. But the other three went with me; all four of us rode bareback to the place where the calf lay.

"There," I said, pointing to him.

Mama was the first to unfork her horse, sliding to the ground where the grass was still dewy wet. As she moved quickly to the dead animal her boots made dark green footprints on the gray quilt of pasture.

Dabney and Lightning followed her.

Mama felt the calf. "Colder than Cain."

"What ails him?" I asked.

Still kneeling, Mama ran her hand over the black hair. "I can't feel no lesions. And there don't seem to be no blood loss. But there's a swelling under his skin. All bloated."

Dab rubbed the dead calf. "It's like he inflated up with gas."

Mama nodded.

"What is it?" Lightning asked.

Feeling the calf all over, Mama looked up at Dabney. Her face was a fright. "It might be black leg."

"No," Dab near to whispered.

"Can ponies catch it?" I asked.

"I don't know." Mama stood up, not very straight, as her shoulders stooped under the news. "I've seed it before, on Herefords. On them it's easier to spot. Legs'll turn to a bluish purple."

Dabney repeated the two words. "Black leg?"

Again my mother nodded, the tired gray in her hair seeming to match the gray of our morning. "Best you ride yourself into Otookee and fetch back Hoolie Swain. He'll know."

Without another word or a saddle, Dab curled

himself up onto Socky and went thundering off to the east until the mist swallowed him. I rode along with Mama and Lightning, and we found a second down calf and then a third.

They looked as poorly as the first.

The third calf we located lay by the swamp's edge; not in water, but only near it. A big black brood cow, the calf's mother, stood nearby, as if waiting for her dead young'n to get up on his feet. With a wave of his hat, Lightning spooked her away with one whoop.

"Hyah!"

It took about half a forever for Mr. Hoolie Swain to get to Spanish Hoof. Because he was so ample built, he never rode a horse; instead, he usual drove a wagon and two mules.

Dab, on Socky, rode alongside.

They found us in the south meadow. Mr. Swain, wearing bib overalls and no shirt, climbed down from his wagon bench, hurried to a fallen calf, and knelt down. His chubby hand stroked the belly fur the wrong way, to peek at the skin. Then, with a grunt that sounded to weigh more than he did, he stood up to face Mama.

"It ain't good, Miz Beecher."

"Black leg?"

"Yes'm. Nary an ounce of doubt."

"How contagious is it?"

Hoolie Swain pulled off his floppy cowboy hat and ragged his ruddy face with a red bandana. Before answering, he wadded it back into a ball, stuffing a pocket.

"It's called a bacteria," he said. "But it ain't total contagious." He held up a warning hand. "I doubt it'll poison your brood cows."

"All the calves?" Mama asked.

Hoolie Swain nodded. "I'd guess every one of 'em."

Dab swore.

"What about the cows now pregnant?" Mama asked Mr. Swain. "Will the unborn calves git stricken?"

"I guess no. And a mature cow or bull don't fall to it much," Hoolie answered Mama. "But I'd say it's black leg for certain. Over the years I seen a passel of cases 'twixt here and Okeechobee. A spate of 'em. All looked exact like this'n." As he spoke Hoolie nudged the black calf with the toe of a boot.

"I can't believe it," said Dabney.

Mr. Hoolie Swain shrugged his big naked shoulders. "You best do, son. Git another opinion if'n ya itch to. Yet I wouldn't waste no time on it. Not when ya risk sickly calves mixing over to your pregnants. What ya best do, Miz Beecher, is to smack a bullet to all them calves. And right sudden. Ya gotta salvation next year's crop."

Dab hung an arm around Mama. As he did it he looked over toward Mr. Hoolie Swain's wagon.

"He brung two rifles, Mama."

Lightning walked to Mama and rested a light

hand on her shoulder. Mama stood like she was dying too.

Dabney wasn't so quiet or contained. Drawing back a boot, he kicked the dead calf. Not hard. It wasn't mean. His face seemed to be yelling that he wanted to kick himself too. Or the whole world.

When I saw Mr. Hoolie Swain go to his wagon for the rifles, I looked at Mama. "No," I said, "ya can't let 'em do it. They mustn't shoot all our beautiful black babies."

Hoolie Swain held a rifle. "It's best. If there was any other way around it . . ."

"Do it," Mama told him.

Chapter 19

I stared at Mama's face.

She looked as if she'd got hammered on an anvil. "It's a sorry shame," said Mama, "to kill what's so young. But I don't guess we'll fritter the day. Dabney, you and Mr. Swain can hold it right here. Load the rifles. Harry, take yourself and your pony back to the house and no fussing about it. And don't worry about Noble. He'll survive healthy."

"Yes'm," I said, starting to turn Noble.

"I'll take Lightning," she said, "and we'll cut the calves back to you two men. So you can do what begs doing."

I rode Noble toward our house. As we neared the shed fence Poker was there in his soiled kitchen apron, waiting for the news. He limped toward me with a questioning face.

"How bad's it?"

I slid off Noble. "Real bad. Hoolie Swain come to examine. It ain't just one calf. We gotta . . . destroy 'em all."

Poke kneeled down to hold me. His face felt whiskery and he smelled of burned breakfast. I could feel the stiff arthritis clumsy his hands as the old man stroked my hair. But he wasn't old or clumsy or smelling to me. He was just Poker. He was all Spanish Hoof. Our luck was his luck. The hurting was his, too.

"I'm frighted, Poke."

"I know."

"It's worse'n when that big ol' gator smelled the birthing blood and then he come an' tore at the mother cow." I was shaking in his arms.

"I know," the old man told me again.

"All our beautiful calves. They gotta git shot because it's black leg. We have to spare the pregnant cows for next season."

"It ain't fair."

"Will the Otookee Bank understand, Poke?"

Somehow, inside me, I was afraid the bank wouldn't care. The old cook couldn't seem to answer me. From the way his arms were shaking, I guessed that Poker was scared too.

I heard a rifle shot.

Even though the sound came from a long ways off, I felt the bullet cut into me. Then I heard shots again. And more. It made me hang tight to Poker, and at the same moment the old man hugged close to me. We just sort of crumpled to each other, listening to the distant crack of the two rifles, as all the calves on Spanish Hoof were dying.

Closing my eyes really tight, I could see Mama

late at night, sitting at our round kitchen table, squinting at all her calf record papers. We wouldn't earn a penny for 1933. Poker held up a corner of his apron to wipe my face dry. As he did it I knew he was trying to be angel gentle.

"We'll make do," he said in a husky voice.

"How?" My voice sounded real unsteady.

Poker bent a tough grin. "I got a few dollars saved up. Maybe not so much. But I don't guess I got too many uses for it. Maybe I was just putting-by for a rainy day, like now."

"Mama's scared too. I saw her face, almost like there was nobody living behind it. She's scared sick."

The old man gave my shoulders a quick shake. "No! She ain't, not Miz Beecher. Why, your ma— if'n a bull gator swum her way and then opened up his big jaws, Miz Beecher would stretch her arm down his throat, all the way inside, grab his tail, and then she'd yank and turn him inside out."

"But the bank—"

Poke shook me again. "Ain't a banker alive or planted that'll spook Violet Beecher. Nary a one. Why, I bet your mother could walk down a lonely road, meet up with Satan hisself, and spit in his eye."

We heard the rifles bark again. They didn't rest. The noise of our calves getting shot went on and on. It felt like a hurtful pain that wouldn't quit its nag.

"Don't you fret," Poke said. "All them banker

ginks in Otookee—they'll know we still got our main herd of brooders. And we got Gertrude too, our bull. Before spring, them brood cows'll all drop healthy calves faster'n rain."

But the way Poker said it made me worry because of the flutter in his voice. It didn't sound like the way he'd cuss at his cookstove. And then kick it. He sounded as if all the sorry was kicking him.

Standing up, Poker wiped my nose with his apron. His face appeared about as twisted as his leg. Like it hurt.

"Wow," he snorted, "I best not squat on that ol' leg of mine no more. She cramps up for certain. Got throwed off a bucker horse, years back. Busted 'er into bits. The rodeo doc that patched me up said I'd never walk again. But I sure fooled that geezer. That's when I become a cook. A stove poker."

I looked up at him. "Is that what your name means? I thought it meant that you played cards a lot." I was trying so hard to talk in my weak voice.

Poke snuffed.

"Well," he admitted with a scratch at his white stubble of beard, "I s'pose I dealt my share at a card table." He held up a crooked finger, as if not to sermon at me but at himself. "Not no more. From now to eternal, I aim to squirrel away my wages. Why, before ya know it, I'll be so rich that I just might fancy myself into town some bright morning and purchase that there Otookee Bank."

Poker wasn't fooling me. I knew that a lot that the

old man was telling me wasn't more than stories. But I didn't rightful care. He patted my eyes and nose again with his apron.

A rifle sounded again.

Poker's hands reached out to cover both of my ears. "Don't listen up," he said. "What we'll do is be happy about next spring's calves. Besides, after I busted myself when I tried to fly off'n a horse, I sure had a black leg."

Poke shook his stiff leg and almost danced it into a sand-kicker of a jig.

"I'm still on my feet, Harry. Ya can't keep a horse from throwin' ya off into dirt and dung. But also, ya can't keep yourself from gittin' back on, to whack the dust off yer britches and mount up again."

"I understand," I told him.

"Sure ya do. Because it ain't no sin to get bucked off. The saddy part comes when a young and healthy rascal looks at life and quits."

Poker hefted me up so's I sit on the top fence rail. He had to grunt to do it.

"Tomorrow night," Poke told me, "I just might scare up a surprise for ya. Honest. It's a genuine honest-to-injun surprise." As he said it Poker crossed his heart, twice, with a bent finger.

"For me?" I tried to sound happy, for Poker's sake, even if I was cracking into busted bits.   .

"Yup. Nobody else. I can't wait myself for y'all to witness it. Maybe you forgot. I didn't. Ya know what day tomorrow be?"

I knew. "It's my birthday." But, saying it, I couldn't figure out how Spanish Hoof would celebrate anything or turn too joyful.

"Right," said Poker. He scratched the back of his neck. "Let's see. I bet you'll be turning eight. Maybe nine."

"Twelve."

"No! A dry-spell squirt like you. Are ya sure?"

"I'm sure." But right now, my age was all I was sure about.

"Good. What say we limp up to the kitchen, you and me, and we'll have a whack at burning the supper?"

"Okay." I jumped down off the fence.

"That's the ol' fight."

As we walked toward the kitchen door I wanted to tell Poker that he didn't have to work so furious at trying to cheer me up. But I kept silent about it. Mainly because I reasoned that the old man was as fretted as I was about how we'd manage to eat this winter. And about what the Otookee Bank people would do once they'd heard the bad news of our herd calves being wiped out.

Poke rested a hand on my shoulder. "We'll make it, Harry. Because, ya see, we ain't just ordinary quitters. Instead, we're all Spanish Hoofers."

"You bet we be," I said, trying to courage it out.

"That's the spirit."

We got to the kitchen door. Poker stopped, looked down at me, and then whipped off his cooking apron. He slipped the white neck-loop over my head, hefted it up some so's it wouldn't drag, and then tied the main string behind my back.

"There ya go, sugar bun. Goodness gravy, but you're looking just exactly like a real genuine cook."

"Do I?" Inside, I didn't care.

Poker nodded his head. "Sure do. But remember one thing, lass. It ain't what ya *wear* that makes who ya be. It's whatcha *do*."

"Okay," I sighed. "Let's go cook."

He opened the door and bowed, allowing me to go into the kitchen first. The smell inside was the same, which made me feel a mite grateful that not everything here at Spanish Hoof had to change. It was an odor of woodsmoke, bacon grease, and a lot of hot cussing.

It all smelled like Poker.

Chapter 20

It was a long day.

At Mama's insist, Mr. Hoolie Swain stayed for supper; and we also made sure that his team of mules got proper fed.

Everyone, except for Poker and me, had tried to wash up before coming to the kitchen table. But they didn't scrub too clean. Their necks still ringed black with smoke from the fires they'd set, away out on the sandy part of our east pasture.

As he was washing, Dab had explained to me how, once shot, the dead calves had to be burned, to kill off any remaining bacteria. So the black leg wouldn't spread.

We were all churchy quiet during the meal. And nobody, even though they hadn't eaten since breakfast, seemed to be very hungered. The four of them had destroyed every one of our calves, dragged their black bodies into a pile, added wood, and set it all aflame.

"Good night to ya, Miz Beecher," said Mr. Swain as he left by the kitchen door.

"I'll be paying you for your time and trouble,

Hoolie," Mama said, "but since we weren't expecting you today, we'll have to ask for credit."

"Don't let it worry you none," Mr. Swain said. "If'n there's anything more I can do, you only gotta ask. You know that."

Mama nodded. "Yes, you're a good friend, Hoolie Swain. I hope we can still be your customers."

He stopped. "By the way, not that I'm offering charity or like that, but if a horse needs shod, or anything, I'll put it on the cuff. Y'all can settle it up after ya git to your feet again. Hear?"

"Thanks," Mama said.

I couldn't allow Mr. Hoolie Swain to leave Spanish Hoof with only a meal to say thanks. So I ran to him. Holding out his big arms, he lifted me high and swung me around.

Mr. Swain was the only one of the six of us who left the kitchen. The rest of us stayed. Poker and I did up the supper dishes, while Mama, Dab, and Lightning sat around the kitchen table. It was plain to read on their faces what kind of a workday they'd put in. Their faces drained to empty.

What made it harder was the fact that it wasn't work for profit. It was only for loss.

"Tomorrow," said Mama, "I best fetch myself to town and pay a call to the Otookee Bank people."

Dab looked at her. "What'll ya say?"

"The truth, son. I'll tell 'em we're down but we ain't out. Not yet. And not ever. But we're close to it."

"We certain ain't," said Poker. "Don't ya fret,

Miz Beecher. I got some cash to invest. Always wanted to own me a wee ol' hunk of Spanish Hoof, but I dassn't to dare ask it. So, right now, I'm asking."

Mama didn't seem able to speak.

Poker went on. "What I'm requesting, Miz Beecher, is sort of this. With all due respect, I'd take it as a honor if you'd allow me to buy myself a acre of Spanish Hoof. The price don't matter a hoo-ha. I aim to purchase as much as I got the scratch to pay ya for. I'll invest every dang penny."

Lightning grinned at Mama. "Yes'm. Me too."

"That ain't the all of it," Poker said. "When I die, I aim to will it all back. It'll be writ down legal and proper. So that Dabney and Harry'll inherit what little I got to bequeath 'em."

Mama slowly smiled and then looked at each of our two hands in turn.

"Poker . . . Lightning . . . it wouldn't be too honest fair. Leastwise, not right today. Your investments might turn to worthless."

Poker kicked the stove. "Miz Beecher, if you'll pardon me for saying it outright, there ain't one blessed article on Spanish Hoof that be worthless. Except for two. Me and this old cusser." He booted the stove again.

"We can't let 'em do it, Mama," said Dabney. "We shouldn't allow 'em to go broke-busted for our sakes."

"Please," said Lightning. "This here's all a home

we got, Miz Beecher. If I can buy me a sliver of it, to own, I'll be content. But if you say no, I be singing 'Sundown' again."

I smiled. It was the most I'd ever heard Lightning say.

"He's right," Poker butted in. "Me and Light, we gotta feel part of it. No, that's wrong. What we need to feel is *all* of it. We gotta be partners of the down as well as the up."

"I've got money too," I said. "In my piggy."

It was Dabney's turn. "Mama," he said, "I been saving up for years to git married. But if we lose the land, I can't ask Trudy Sue to live at *her* place. So best I throw in with y'all."

My mother was powerful busy, twisting her head to look at one of us, then another. It was sort of spooky, seeing Mama have so little to say. Then, all she could manage to blurt out was only two words. "My family."

"We sure are," said Poker.

"But," Mama said, "before us Beechers take your savings, we oughta think on it for a spell. Please understand."

Poke nodded.

Holding up her open palm, Mama softly spoke. "The five of us," she said. "We're like the fingers on a hand." Her fingers were still wide apart. "Alone," she said, "we're not very strong. But together"—she closed her fingers into a tight fist—"we're one zinger of a team."

Outside, the wind had changed.

My nose wrinkled at the odor. It come from the southeast, from the fires, a smell of dead calves burning. The screen door of the kitchen was open, and Poker limped over to close the bigger door. He looked at my mother.

"It's a sadder of a stink, Miz Beecher. But maybe part of it is the finger of the Lord, to tap us on our shoulders. And remind us that we ain't never to quit, or holler uncle."

"Never," said Dab. But his voice sounded beaten, the way my mother's face looked. Dirty and down.

Later, down beside the bunkhouse, Poker tended to one of the bathtubs he'd bought in Otookee and heated some water so Lightning could git hisself scrubbed.

"Maybe it's the end," I heard the old man grumble. "And once them banker boys git a whiff of burning calves, Spanish Hoof'll be washed up too." Poke kicked the tub with his boot.

Mama took her bath inside. So did Dabney. Nobody talked a whole lot to anyone else. Mouths were too tuckered out for words.

As soon as the darksome come I sat on the front stoop and looked out across the land. The fires were still burning, giving off their eye-smarty smoke and smell.

Mama didn't come downstairs.

Dabney did. But he was wearing only his pajama trousers. As he leaned a bare shoulder against a porch post, looking out at the orange fires, his body seemed to whisper one word. *Whipped.*

"Dab," I said, "I'm sure wishing there was something I could do to ease Mama."

He nodded, staring up at the moonlight. "I know. There will be. Pretty soon, you'll be up-enough growed to assist her on calf records. But we ain't got any calves to keep tabs on. Nary a single one left."

I got up to stand beside him. He sure had stretched up this summer. I had me a secret hunch that it was Trudy Sue Ellsworth who made Dab sprout up so sudden tall. But maybe it was more. Perhaps it was taking care of Spanish Hoof, knowing that ranching was wearing down our mother. Then he turned to me like he could read my thoughts.

"Mama's out straight," he said.

"Asleep?"

"I wish. When I took a peek into her room, she was stretched out on her bed in her bathrobe, staring at the ceiling. Didn't once look at me. Sure hope she can spark up enough guts for Otookee, come morning."

I scratched the back of my head. "What do you think she'll tell 'em at the bank?"

Before answering, Dab wrapped both his arms around his own chest, almost as if he'd become cold on a hot evening. His eyes looked at me as though I wasn't even to home.

"Violet Beecher'll play it straight," he said.

"Mama's not like some folks. She won't beg on charity. Not our mother. She'll speak right up and say it all honest. At the worst, maybe we'll have to put up some of our land for a tax sale."

"No," I said. "We can't sell off Spanish Hoof. It's our home, Dab. We *live* here."

"Times are hard, Harry."

As he said it, I recalled what old Cheater McCabe had answered, the morning last May when he'd brought me Noble. So I said the same to my brother because, somehow, it held reason.

"Times always were."

Dab sort of grinned. "You're right about that. Mama's never knowed a *easy* time. Not once in her whole blessed life. She wouldn't know *easy* if'n it come up and kicked her shins."

"Dab," I said, "I reckon that tonight I'm fixing to slip in and sleep with Mama. I just can't allow her to sleep lonesome. Not tonight."

My brother nodded. "Good notion."

Chapter 21

"How do I look? Presentable?"

"Like a really rich lady," I told her. "Smarter than a queen."

Mama was in her dark church dress, even though it wasn't Sunday. Lightning had hitched up Golly to the wagon for Mama's trip into Otookee to visit the bank.

"I'm dolled up because it's Harry's birthday," she said. "Not for bankers."

Dabney and I, along with Poker and Lightning, all stood around near the door to our barn, to give Mama a proper sendoff. The worry lines on her face sort of said that she wasn't looking forward to the journey. It wasn't to favor going in to church service.

"If'n it was up to me," said Dab, "I'd say you certain do look like one prosperous rancher lady."

Poke nodded. "Pretty as pie."

Holding up an edge of her skirt with one hand, Mama climbed up onto the wagon bench and sat herself in a position to handle Golly's ribbons.

"Maybe the dress weren't such a nifty idea," she said. "I just oughta sit a saddle instead of a wagon and look like I usual do."

"No," I told her. "Them banker fellas all march around in black suits. So, the way I got it figured, they'd be spooked to see a lady in jeans."

Clutching the reins into one fist, Mama nodded at me. "Yes, they probable would. It sure be a waste of a good workday to sashay into a bank and argue ranching talk with a pack of empty suits."

She just sat the wagon bench, appearing to me as though she didn't much care going. I noticed how her eyes squinted east, toward Otookee.

"Nope," she final said, "I made a mistake to gussy up thisaway. I'd do better in my work pants. And them bankers would look more natural in dresses."

Poke hooted, slapping his leg. "Bless ya, Miz Beecher. I'd wager that you could squeeze pleasure from a prune."

Mama shot Poker a grin. "Well, best I git headed before the place closes fer the day and all them banker gents trot home to iron their undies."

As Mama clucked to Golly and slapped the ribbons, the wagon creaked forward, its turning wheels cutting dark stripes into the Florida sand.

"Stay clear of Nell's Place," Poke warned, and it near to turned me inside out with laughing.

"I'll try to."

"Give 'em holy, Mama," said Dabney. But his grin faded back to a line that looked firm and hard.

136

Poker pulled out his harmonica and busted into "Zip Coon," while Lightning and I hooked our arms together, dancing a circle. Dab waved his cowboy hat in the air until Mama final looked back over her shoulder to return the wave. The four of us just sort of stood there, watching the wagon shrink into its own dust, passing under the distant poles that held up our SPANISH HOOF sign.

"She'll do dandy," said Poker.

Dabney let out a tired sigh. "Maybe," he said.

Poker rubbed a dry mouth with the back of one crooked hand. "I could sure handle me a spirity drink right about sudden," said the old cook.

I punched him. "You do," I told him, "and I'll order Dab and Lightning to haul you over to the swamp and feed ya to a gator."

Poker felt his chin. "Well now, I didn't confess all that too serious. Besides, today's too special a day, in case ya up'n forgit."

"I know," I said to Poker. "It's my birthday."

"Nah," said Dab. "Must be a mistake about all that. Girls don't git birthdays. Ain't a gal alive who'd ever cotton up to admit she's having one."

I tried to sock Dabney. But then Poker snuck his dirty old apron over my head so's I couldn't see to kick anybody. To make it all worse, Lightning and Dab tickled me close to dying while I was hollering to beg 'em all to quit up.

"Okay," said Dab. "Fun's over. So best we all crack into a day's work and have at it."

Poker limped toward the kitchen.

Taking shovels, a water jug, and two horses, Dabney and Lightning rode out to the southeast meadow where last evening's fires were still smoking. I followed along on Noble. Nobody talked a whole bit. What we saw was too hurtful sad to add words.

The smell still hung in the air, along with little plumes of smoke, a heavy morning stink of death. It was as though somebody mean, old Mr. Black Leg, had set fire to Spanish Hoof and burned us all to ashes. The fire piles were gray. Here and there, I could spot the remains of a dead calf. I don't guess I ever took a notice of a sadder sight.

"Noble," I said in a whisper, "I'm sure thankful that ponies don't fall to black leg, the way calves do."

Lightning and Dab hustled their shovels out there on the sandy place for most of the day. The heat of the fires roasted both of them to a gritty sweat. Shirts off, they scattered the gray ash and then dug hole after hole to bury the carcasses.

Noble and I watched.

Sometimes Dab and Lightning would stop for water or for some no-smoke breathing. That's when I'd grab me a shovel and dig too. A heaping spade of sand hefted to be a lot more than I figured. But I picked the smallest half-burned calf, dug a hole for him, and then finished my job. It hurt my hands, yet I wanted to see it through, and the two other workers let me go it alone until I finished.

Somehow, they must've knowed how important it was for me to handle a job by my lonesome. Because the little calf I buried was the one we saved from the swamp gator, one I'd fed from a bottle. Also for the reason that today was my birthday.

"I ain't eleven no more," I told 'em.

Dab grinned at me. "You sure ain't, Harry. You can outwork any growed man in Florida and at least half the women."

"Honest?"

Lightning smiled too. "I never seen a man or a mule work no harder."

The smell of the burning and dying was starting to scorch the inside of my nose, like I was about fixing to choke. Or to upchuck. Inside my belly, there sure wasn't too much to chuck up, seeing as the three of us didn't stop for a noon meal. A chore like the one we'd performed didn't really serve up much of an appetite.

Not even Dabney mentioned chow.

After our job was polished off, we somehow couldn't leave the place. We just stood there, staring at all the ashes and the fresher, darker sand. Somewhere, under it all, was our herd of calves. I wanted somebody to say something. Or maybe pray.

Lightning started to hum. It was a soft little song, with no words necessary to trim it fancy.

A hum that sounded more of a breeze than music.

Chapter 22

"Mama's home."

Dabney said the two words as we were riding home from our calf burying, but I must've been near asleep and almost fell off Noble. Dab, who was riding in front of me, pointed to our wagon which was back from Otookee.

Dab nudged Socky into a trot; beside us, Lightning kept up with our eager pace.

"I gotta know what happened," Dab said.

"Me too," I told him.

Lightning busied himself pulling off saddles, while Dab and I ran toward the house. Poker met us at the door. With a sober expression on his face, our cook held up a twisted finger over his mouth to beg quiet.

"She's upstairs," he said, "resting."

"Anything serious?" Dab asked Poke.

The old man shrugged his shoulders. "Well, I ain't no doctor. But her face sure looked wrung out to me."

Nobody mentioned the Otookee Bank or asked

any money questions. It didn't seem so sudden important, not compared to Mama's health.

As we charged into Poker's kitchen he said, "Doc Strong brung her home. I got me a hunch that maybe Miz Beecher paid him a visit in town. Before leaving, he said your ma best tackle life a step or so slower."

Without another word, Dabney and I stomped up the stairs to Mama's room. Dab went first. I had a fright in my stomach.

"She's sleeping," he whispered to me.

"No, I ain't," Mama answered.

For some reason, as we entered her room Dab took off his cowboy hat. Maybe it was to show respect to Mama. But the gesture gave me a funny feeling in my throat. Dabney stood on one side of her bed. I stood on the other. Mama was in her nightgown. Her head was on her pillow, but she sort of rolled it back and forth, looking at each of us in turn.

"My two rascals," she said.

"What happened?" Dabney asked her.

"Nothing."

"Poker just told us," I said, "that Doc Strong come all the way home with ya. So you best not blanket it over with a story."

Dab gently sat on the edge of the bed in order to touch Mama's hand. His weight made the springs complain.

"I s'pose," Mama told us in a low voice, "you

want to learn about what the Otookee Bank had to say. Not much cheerful."

My brother shook his head. "Never mind about the bank," he said. "We'd like to study on what Doc Strong had to say, and we want it straight out."

"What's wrong in you, Mama?" I asked.

Without answering, Mama reached up both her skinny arms to pull Dabney and me down close to her. The cotton of her white nightie rubbed soft against my cheek. I kept waiting for her to tell us things, about why Doc Strong come home with her.

"I'll crawl downstairs for the celebration supper," she said, "even if I gotta rip my ribs trying."

The hardness seemed gone from her voice, as if Otookee had sapped away all of her spirit. Or most of it. I couldn't understand how come the toughest person in the world had sudden turned so puny. Her words seemed to hang like a wet flag.

"From now on," she said, "I don't guess I'll be able to handle my full share of the ranch work. Doc says I gotta treat my heart like it's always Sunday."

Dab raised his head to look at her. His face seemed to be telling her that he'd work double. Even triple. He wasn't a boy anymore. Now he'd have to be a growed man.

"I'm sorry," Mama told us.

My brother's voice whispered deep and sturdy to her. "There ain't a need for sorry. The four of us'll pull weight." As he said it I saw his fingers tighten on hers.

"You never told us what Doc Strong done," I said. "Did he operate?"

"No, child." Mama sort of smiled, shaking her head. "You've already started to command the mending now, so there's one thing to learn."

"What's that?"

"Ya don't patch up a rag."

Dab stood up. "You ain't no rag, Mama."

I felt her hand easing in mine. "Well now, if *wore out* be a measure . . ." Her voice melted away, as though she didn't have the strength to sprinkle salt.

"You look so tired," I told Mama, "and pale."

Again she tried a smile. "If there's a job more tuckering than ranching," she said, "it's banking."

"Forgit the bank," Dabney said. "You won't have to journey in there no more with a hat in your hand, to beg."

Mama looked up at him through eyes that were barely half open. "What'll we do, son?"

Her question surprised me more'n a mite. Because my mother wasn't the make of person to ask what prodded doing. Miz Violet Beecher usual *told*.

Dab cleared his throat. Then, as he spoke, his voice sunk deeper into his chest. "We each got us a job. But the only single chore *you* got is resting up. Yours is to retire."

"Retire? Me?"

"Yes'm."

Dabney and I, along with Lightning's help, had worked in dirt all day. Coming home, neither of us had bothered to whoa at Poker's sink to wash up. So, as I looked down, I spotted a few grains of grit on Mama's hand, where I'd touched her.

"Here," I said, pulling my wadded bandana from a hip pocket of my jeans, "I soiled your hand, Mama. I got ya some dirty."

She pulled away her hand.

"Leave it on me, Harry."

"Why?"

"Because it's Spanish Hoof." Eyes closed, her fingers lightly curled to caress the specks of grit. "It ain't dirt. It's home."

Dab looked across the bed at me. "Maybe," he said, "we best let her take sleep. We'll come upstairs for her whenever Poker announces he's final burnt supper."

The two of us crept on tiptoe out of Mama's bedroom and went quietly down the wooden stairs. We sat out front on the porch step, to talk.

"We oughta pay Doc Strong," said Dabney. "He's a right decent guy to give up most a afternoon to trek away out here and then back to Otookee."

"Do we got the money?" I asked.

"You was in bed asleep last night," Dab told me, whirling his cowboy hat around in tiny circles. "Mama and me checked our figures and totals."

"Are we poor?"

He punched my shoulder. "Heck no, we ain't poor. All we be is broke-busted."

"But we still gotta pay folks. It just wouldn't set right to cheat people."

Dab put his beat-up old hat on my head. "We'll pay, Harry. We won't ask for no free ride from nobody. But we owe Hoolie Swain and Doc. Other bills too."

"How we gonna pay up?"

My brother sighed. "I already decided. If you agree to it, we oughta sell off some of our stock. A few of our brood cows."

"Okay."

Dab said, "We gotta git us some cash money to square matters. I didn't ask Mama if she squeaked us a loan from the bank. I already know she struck out. Her face spoke it all. Somehow, we gotta hang on to Spanish Hoof because it'll one day be Mama's monument."

"Will the cows bring enough?"

Dab shook his head. "Because they're pregnant oughta help out. But we still best unload other stock too."

"Such as?"

"Horses. I could sell off Socky and pull in a handsome dollar for him."

I couldn't breathe. All I could wonder about was how I could help Dab keep his horse. And then the answer hollered into my ear.

"Maybe," I said, "I'll sell Noble."

As I said it, really soft, I wanted Dabney to argue

about it, to tell me straight out how fooly it would be. Yet he didn't. All he did was hang a heavy arm around my neck. He didn't have to mumble me an answer. Maybe because he knew how the truth of it could cut me.

"You'll need Socky to work the ranch," I told Dab. I made myself say it.

As I spoke my eyes closed to recall the dirt specks that Mama didn't want wiped off her hand. The remembering how Mama looked, in bed upstairs, caused me to pull away from Dab's arm, stand up, and stamp my foot. Then I felt like a simple fool doing it. Like a dumb little kid.

"We gotta hang on to Spanish Hoof," I said.

My brother stared at me. "You know what you are, Harry?"

"Don't say it. I'm being a *limit* again."

"No," he said. "You're sort of my big sister."

Chapter 23

"Blind her eyes," Poker said.

"Okay," said Dab, getting up from the supper and walking around the kitchen table to station himself behind me and cover my eyes with both hands. I could hardly sit still.

"I'm real ready," I said.

Somewhere, in one corner of the kitchen, I heard the scratching of matches getting lit; along with a bicker, in whispers, between Poke and Lightning. So I just sat quiet to the table and pretended I didn't know what was up.

"And no peeking," ordered Poke.

I heard our cook limping my way. It seemed to take near to a hundred years.

"Open your eyes," said Dab.

On the table in front of me sat a beauty of a white cake, with HARRY lettered across the frosting; plus, I counted, twelve pink little candles. All lit up and spitting tiny flickers. As I sucked in a full helping of air, puckering my lips to blow, Poker said, "Hold it. First ya gotta make a wish, Harry."

I looked at Mama, sitting at our kitchen table in her faded bathrobe, which appeared as wore out as its owner. She'd know what I'd be wishing. So would everyone else. I wished. But not for a saddle, as I had planned all summer. Besides, I knew that Noble was my present in advance, last May; so I'd be greedy to ask for more. Except to keep Noble.

Then, just so's not to ruin all the joyful, I said, "Last year, when I was only eleven, I was wishing for a pony. So I know that a birthday wish certain do come to true." It hurt to say it.

"Ya ain't supposed to *tell*," said Poker.

"It's *my* birthday," I said, "so I can wish and tell anything I want to. Isn't that right, Mama?"

I read her smile. Even though the deep lines on Mama's face seemed to say that she was beyond wishing.

"All I want," I said, "is a ample lot more birthday parties, just like tonight, right here to Spanish Hoof."

Everybody clapped as I blew out the candles, and Poke yelled out a *"Yahoo!"*

Dab handed me a long knife. I carved the cake into five hunks, trying to be as fair as possible so's Dab wouldn't hog the giant of the litter.

He didn't. Instead, he just sat there acting church righteous and was the last person to grab a plate of cake. He sure was a changing guy. All growed up to manhood. Taller every day. Yet now it was his face, not his frame, that seemed to be stretching. I was glad he'd bothered to shave his thirteen whiskers before supper.

"Here's to ya, Harry," said Poker, jabbing his fork into the white meat of the cake, hefting up three mouthfuls in one trip.

"*Dee*-licious," said Dab.

It sure was. "Thanks," I said. "It's powerful good."

"Oughta be," Poke told us. "I cracked ten eggs inta that there masterpiece. And near to a bucket of sugar."

"It's sweeter than Christmas," I told Poker.

The old cook leaned across our table to pinch my cheek. "Twelve," he said, shaking his head. "Don't seem possible. Ya only got born last Tuesday, seems like."

Lightning said nothing. Only ate. Yet he'd look my way over every bite, allowing his eyes to glisten me a Happy Birthday.

"Mama," I asked, "what did I look like when I final got myself born?"

"Ugly," said Dab. "All red and pink-blotchy. I saw ya. In fact, the minute ya got hatched, you looked so awful ugly that Doc Strong slapped Mama."

Even I had to grin away that one. And I thought Poke, Lightning, and Dab were near about to choke on laughter. I liked it best when Mama smiled. Her eyes were telling me that she remembered my birth.

"Maybe," said Poker, "I put in too much sugar."

"Not enough," Lightning told him.

In a soft voice Mama asked Poker whether or not he had his harmonica with him.

"Yes'm, Miz Beecher, I brung it up from the bunkhouse." He patted the pocket of his blue shirt. "Got it handy."

"Good," said Mama, "because I think we all oughta sing 'Happy Birthday to You.' "

"To *me*?" Poke asked her with a wink.

"No," said Dabney, "to Golly Mule."

"Fine with me," said Poke. "I'll just scoot out to the pasture, locate Golly, and blow her a tune."

Actually I wasn't allowed to sing the song, it being my birthday and all; yet I sang louder than anyone else. As I was singing I tried to force my face to smiling, and not remember about all the sadness that might be coming due. I even tried some not to always look at Mama. Instead, I attempted seeing her ride a horse at a full let-out gallop, standing the stirrups, guiding reins with a easy hand.

We got to the part in the song that was "Happy Birthday, dear Harry," but Dab made sure to sing "Harriet" instead.

Funny, but I didn't care a hoot. I was willing to be Harriet Beecher, because that was what Mama had named me. So it'd have to fit me proper. I'd been named, she'd said, after a very famous lady, a poet or something, whose name had been Harriet Beecher Stowe. Mama also said that, years back, President Lincoln met her personal, shook hands, and said, "So this is the little lady that started this great war." As to which war it exactly was, I didn't clear recall.

I heard a *pop* sound!

Looking around, I saw Poker and Lightning both holding tight to the biggest green bottle I ever saw. White foam was squirting out its steamy neck, and a cork bounced off the wall, ceiling, then on the table. The cork came to a rest on our empty chicken platter.

"Ya didn't," Mama told Poker.

Lightning flashed teeth. "He did."

"Just a sip for each of the one of us, Miz Beecher," pleaded Poke, holding one paper cup and dropping four. "It's a kinda special event. You know why."

There was a hurried look that passed between Poke and Mama, a quick little blink of a glance that told me how Poke knew about everything, yet he didn't want to fan Mama's ire. Mama, I knew, didn't approve of spirits. Certainly not a drop for Dabney or for me. That's why I was so electric jolted when I saw her hands clap.

"Oh," said Mama, "what the deuce."

"It's genuine champagne," said Poke.

"Honest," said Lightning. "We purchased it special in town last Saturday night."

Poke slopped the champagne into the little cups, while Lightning and Dab busied themselves getting the first one over to Mama. Then to themselves.

"Don't I git a taste too?" I asked.

Mama nodded. "One cup of it. And that is absolutely all." Never had I seen Mama take a drink. But she lifted her little cup high over the table and then stood up. We raised our cups too. "Gentlemen," she said, meaning Dab, Poke, and Lightning, "I hereby propose a toast to my daughter, Miss Harriet Beecher, on the occasion of her twelfth birthday."

We all hollered.

"Cheers," said Mama.

As I took my first sip of genuine champagne, expecting it to burn the way people claimed jug brandy did, I got a smooth surprise. There wasn't much taste to it. In fact, it sort of favored that citrate of magnesia that Mama dosed me for constipation.

"It's medicine," I said. The word sort of crept up through the herd of bubbles that were teasing my nose.

"In that case," said Mama, lifting her cup once again, "I certain hope it works."

It was the best birthday party that I'd ever celebrated, surely better than the earlier eleven. I was tempted to dump the rest of my champagne into a bucket, to share with Noble; but Mama advised me against it.

"Animals got too much reason," she said. "And if I got any, I ought to chase upstairs to bed."

Then she excused herself, got up from the kitchen

---

table, yanked the belt of her ratty bathrobe a hitch snugger, and paraded upstairs. Dab assisted her.

Lightning and Poke battled the dishes. I helped clear. Left over on Mama's meal plate was a half-gnawed chicken bone. I knew it was a wing. Nobody else ever took a wing off a platter if'n there was better to grab. Only my mother.

Going to sleep that night, I tried to feel brave. Yet it wasn't too cinchy. Outside my window a moon was doing its best to cheer up Spanish Hoof with a silver light. Bugs were out celebrating too. It was a going-to-bed music that I'd heard every night of my entire life.

"Bugs," my mother sometimes said, "are the curse of a kitchen but the choir to a evening." I could hear her saying it.

I rolled over. Now I'd turned twelve, I was thinking, it was time to stretch up, like Dab. Not only tall. It'd be proper for me somehow to do more stuff on Spanish Hoof, so we'd prosper again.

What made my hands grip my bedsheet really hard was when I thought about Noble.

Chapter 24

I helped Dabney milk Ruthie.

"You're getting it," Dab had told me. "Now that you're twelve, your milking talents will improve real sudden. You'll see."

"Thanks," I said.

As I watched Dab leave on Socky to ride fence, to the west, I couldn't understand how gentle he'd become. He was near to human. Maybe not as sweet and quiet as Lightning, but doggone close. Lately he'd turned so helpful that, at times, I almost forgot he was my brother.

Right after we'd finished eating Poke's breakfast, Dab told me that there wasn't no work for me to handle today. He'd suggested that I go spend time with my pony.

"Harry," he'd said to me, "there's to be a . . . a *deciding* soon, and it'll be one that you'll sort of have to make on your own hook. I can't decide for you."

"What's it about?" I'd asked.

Dabney sighed. "Noble."

It hurt plentiful to hear it. Yet I knew it was going to happen. So I headed on foot toward the east meadow, where Noble usual grazed and slept. All of our critters were outdoor animals, even Ruthie.

"Noble?" I called.

When I couldn't see him, I started to run, worrying some about black leg. In spite of the fact that Hoolie Swain had told us that ponies and mature cows couldn't catch the disease. Still and all, Hoolie might've been wrong.

I yelled out again. "Noble!"

Then I saw him. His ears were pointed up, and he was trotting around a low clump of palmetto, coming my way. I ran to him and wrapped both arms around his warm neck. There was no way on earth that I could explain to him about how hurtful the black leg had hit us. And how near we were to being money broke.

"Times are tough, Noble. So maybe we all gotta grow tougher, to save Spanish Hoof for Mama. Because she's took ill and stays resting in bed now."

It was true. But sometimes, really late at night, I'd wake up and listen to her talking to my brother, going over deeds and papers. Last night I'd sneaked downstairs, keeping mouse quiet, to look inside the shoe box where our important papers got kept. I lit a kerosene lamp to squint at them. But they certain didn't add up to ample sense for me. Just a bunch of numbers and words.

On one of the papers that I unfolded I read "Otookee Bank" and the word "mortgage." None of it was simple to understand, so I'd just blowed out the lamp and crept back upstairs to my bed.

"Noble," I said, "it's time you knew that I ain't

155

eleven anymore. I got myself to be twelve now, and I can't be no kid on a pony. I best start helping out in every way I can handle, the way Trudy Sue does, over at the Ellsworths'."

He tossed his handsome head. It was like Noble was waiting for me to grab his mane, the way Dabney had instructed, and kick a leg over his back. But I somehow didn't want to ride him today. Leastwise, not yet. Because now certain wasn't a time for enjoying.

Lowering his head, Noble bit into a clump of grass, pulled his head up again, and chewed. How, I was wondering, could I ever say so long to such a wonderful pet?

"Losing a pony," I said to Noble, "maybe ain't as painful sorry as a whole family losing a ranch and a home. But it certain is sorry enough."

Noble switched his tail, stinging my face; and for some reason I didn't full understand, I wanted it to hurt me. Real bad.

"I ain't going to cry, Noble. You hear? Even if it's the Depression and the Otookee Bank people—"

As I stood on our meadow along with my pony, whispering a lot of my secret thoughts into his soft ear, I wondered if ponies ever cry. Well, if they didn't, they certain were stronger than I was, right now.

"I don't understand," I was telling him. "It sort of seems like we was holding on proper, then we dropped it all. And if things turn worse, we'll have to sell other parts of us. More brood cows, and maybe Dabney'll even trade away Socky. And we'll sell Ruthie too. Maybe we then can't pay wages to Poker and Lightning—"

My arms hung around Noble's neck, like I was trying to hang on to everything and to everybody I knew. It was time to be brave. Trouble is, I was reasoning, nobody ever taught me how. Maybe bravery was being able to say good-bye to treasures.

"I don't guess I can do it, Noble."

Bending over, the way Hoolie Swain had showed me, I hefted up one of Noble's hoofs, to inspect it. To do it made me feel older. Sort of like I was growed up and was turning, as Dabney said, responsible. Looking at the underside, I could notice how Noble's hoof had growed too and would need to get shaved.

"Noble," I said, holding his hoof between my knees like a regular blacksmith, "it ain't fair to invite Hoolie to sweat over a fire and hammer hot iron, then not pay him his due in cash money."

Beef calves, according to how Dabney had explained it, was Spanish Hoof's only money crop. We didn't have no citrus groves or raise produce. But this coming fall, there wouldn't be no calves to ship. And no money coming in.

As I released his hoof I told Noble, "If you can't understand about the calves and the mortgage, you ain't alone. I don't guess I understand it complete. All I know is we got ourselfs bills to pay and no money to fork over to people we owe."

There was a brown thistle burr in Noble's tail.

Working it loose sure did pricker my fingers, yet I felt righteous doing it for my pony. Because, soon, Noble wouldn't be mine. He'd get ridden by another kid. Leaning against Noble, closing my eyes shut tight, I could sort of vision a little girl, like me, on Noble's back, seated where my hands now stroked him gentle.

"Soon," I told him, "you won't be Noble no longer." His next owner, I figured, will cotton to give a new pony a new name. "I can only hope that some lucky kid learns about you, the way I done, and picks up your hoofs to check matters. Sprays you with Flit. And pulls the thistle burrs out of your tail."

As Dabney had suggested, I spent most of my day with Noble. Just the pair of us, alone. It was strange not to ride him; but for some odd reason, I didn't want to use him none. Instead, all I wanted to do was to sort of hold him in my arms. Together, Noble and I walked to the places where I'd earlier rode him, strolling side by side, to say good-bye to the palmetto and live oak and the swamp. I didn't have to lead him. Because everywhere I walked, he tagged along behind, keeping close and sometimes nudging me with his soft pestery nose.

I'd promised myself, and Noble, that I wouldn't cry. But I don't guess I was quite as brave as somebody twelve ought to be.

I knew Noble couldn't tell that, somewhere inside, I was part eleven.

Chapter 25

"Mr. Guthrie's come," said Dabney.

The two of us walked out the front door of the house as his truck pulled in at Spanish Hoof. I hated looking at it. And I didn't take to its driver much warmer.

"Morning," said Dab.

He shook hands with Mr. Sam Guthrie. "This here's Harry, my sister. She's to come along with us, if'n it's okay. We're partners."

Mr. Guthrie nodded. "Let's git *to* it. Because I don't got all day to dicker."

Earlier, my brother had rounded up two of our horses—Mama's, plus a gray. I'd brung in Noble.

"We got only them three for sale," said Dab.

Hearing him say it cut into me worse than a ice pick.

Mr. Guthrie walked himself over to the fence, shot the gate latch, and eased inside. Both our horses and Noble looked at him wide-eyed, knowing he was a stranger and not somebody who belonged here at Spanish Hoof. Dab and I followed along. I couldn't feel my feet walking. It was like trying to run during a bad dream.

"They're all prime," said Dab. "And all three's been took gracious care of. Hoolie Swain comes regular to cut their hoofs and to shod 'em."

The horse man didn't answer. Instead, he shot Dabney a glance, as though to say he'd judge his own price. I saw him glide a hand along the back of the gray gelding, then he was feeling each leg. After hefting up every hoof, he marched around front, checking ears and curling back lips to study the gray's teeth. His face turned sour as he looked at Dab and me.

"This horse ain't no colt," he said.

Dabney had warned me, earlier, that a spate of down-talk would be part of the business of trading. It sure was. And I was hating every word Mr. Guthrie said.

"His name's Misty," I said. "He's real gentle. I know because I rode him some before I got my pony." I figured I'd toss in my own up-talk to even the score a mite. Even though all I'd claimed wasn't quite true. Misty could be a bucker.

I tried hard not to look at Noble.

"These days," Mr. Guthrie told us, "horses don't bring a fat price. Besides, I gotta profit my own self a dollar or two."

"Reckon," said Dab. "That's only fair."

Mr. Guthrie examined Mama's horse as he'd done

on the gray. "The horse market," he said, "sure ain't what she once were. Times are tough."

"S'pose so," Dab told him. "Yet I figure there's always a few folks in Florida who be wanting a horse that's got well cared for. Like our three."

The man sighed. As he gave our three animals a disgusted glance he walked around in a circle, looking at Dabney and me, as though he knew we were hard up for cash money. I wanted to grab Noble and gallop away, and keep going forever. Or maybe hide.

"The price of a horse, boy, ain't got a lick to do with what the owner values. All it be is what some other gent, or lady, is willing to cough up. Get me?"

Dab nodded. All I could do was swallow, over and over.

Not being able to hold myself back, I walked over to Noble, to put both my arms around his neck and inhale his sweet pony smell. I hadn't brung a carrot out of Poke's vegetable garden, like usual. Yet my pony didn't seem to be upset over it. Noble just kept on staring at Mr. Guthrie, as though he knew something was dreadful wrong.

I tried to tighten my guts, but there was a warm feeling behind my eyes that burned worse'n a branding fire. It felt like I was fighting everything in the whole world.

Mr. Guthrie walked toward Noble and me.

"Move away, girl," he ordered me. "So's I can fetch me a look at your animal."

"His name's Noble," I said, trying to forget he'd soon get named something new by somebody else.

"If'n I can't sell him," the man said, giving Noble a fish eye, "his name'll be Crow Bait."

"He's my sister's pony," Dab said. "He's a right-eous good little animal, and he means a precious lot to her, Mr. Guthrie. So I'll thank ya not to run him down on sorry talk."

Mr. Guthrie squinted at Dabney. "Bless me," he final said, "but you Beechers sure got some peacock ways. I don't gotta git told *you're* Violet Beecher's boy." He spat to the dust.

"Do you know Mama?" I asked.

The horse man nodded his hat. "Yup, I knowed her for some years. There's a ample of tough bark on 'er too."

Dab sort of grinned. "Thanks," he said. "I'll tell Mama you recall her."

"Years back," Mr. Guthrie went on to say, "your ma traded me a mare. Beauty to look at. Fact was, your ma was a beauty herself at the time. Violet never told me that this pretty mare was somehow right-mounted. So I bought her as a present for my wife's nephew, Eddy. He was a cusser of a boy who weren't worth squat."

"What happened?" Dab asked him.

Mr. Guthrie pulled a pouch of Red Man from his

pocket, selected a wad, then installed the pinch to chaw inside his left cheek. It bulged his ruddy face. To me, it made his mean face meaner.

"Eddy cinched a saddle to her. Then, on the left like usual, he tried to climb aboard. That right-mounted critter shook him around the way a terrier'll shake a rat. Made ol' Eddy eat a healthy swaller of Florida."

"That's too bad," I said. But I didn't feel too sorry.

"Oh, I enjoyed it," said Mr. Guthrie. "The best part was when my wife, Eunice, didn't speak at me for most of a month."

"I don't recall that horse," said Dab.

"No," he said, "you wouldn't. Like I said early, this business deal was years ago. But I do recall Violet Beecher. So tell 'er I still owe the lady either a skinning or a favor."

Mr. Guthrie let a brown stream of tobacco juice squirt from his mouth toward a botfly that had landed on a fence rail. He missed, but that fly sure took off sudden. Watching, I was wishing that Noble and I could be flies.

Saying no more, Mr. Sam Guthrie twisted his body around to complete his look at my pony. Noble tossed his head and moved away a step or two. His ears lay back as he eyed Mr. Guthrie.

"He spook easy?" the man asked me.

"No," I said, moving close to Noble. "He's real

gentle. I ride him with no saddle." I almost told him that we couldn't afford a saddle, but it didn't make no bargaining sense to sound poor.

"Yeah?"

"Honest. All the time."

"Show the man," Dab said.

Throwing a leg over Noble, I trotted him around in a circle, guiding him the way Dabney had taught me to ride, with knee squeeze, plus a gentle hand to his mane.

"You sit good," Mr. Guthrie told me.

"It ain't me," I said. "It's because Noble's so sweetsome that he wouldn't throw off nobody. Not even your cusser nephew." Inside, I was praying that Eddy wouldn't get Noble. Or anybody with a mean manner. The man smiled. And I hated seeing it.

"Well," he said, "I'm near ready to talk money, boy. And I'll do you Beechers a favor an' purchase all three."

"Good," said Dab.

My throat hurt. I was hard hoping that Mr. Guthrie would only want to buy our pair of horses. Even though it wasn't too easy to trade away Mama's favorite or say good-bye to Misty.

Dabney and Mr. Guthrie had walked over toward the gate and were busy on chatter about price. The man was shaking his head; Dab held up fingers and appeared to look sweaty.

Mr. Guthrie just spitted his juice.

"Okay," I said to Noble, still sitting on his warm back, "you're to have a new home. Maybe you'll git another little girl who ain't quite up-growed to a woman yet, like me, to love you and yank up carrots for you." As I spoke I held my chin up high.

Noble shook his head. Not that he understood what I was telling him. I knew he just sort of done it, like usual.

"Noble," I said, near to choking, "please remember Spanish Hoof a mite, if a pony can recall a good home. I'll tell Golly and Ruthie that you'll miss 'em a lot. They'll miss you, too. Mama's in bed. She don't know we're selling off stock. Dab don't want to worry her none. You understand."

I hoped he did, even though I couldn't force myself to tell my pony how much I'd miss him. And how broke my heart would be. It was near all I could do to climb off Noble for the final time, and I hid my face against Dab's shirt. Eyes closed, I heard Mr. Guthrie load the two horses, and then Noble, up a ramp and into his truck. I didn't give Noble a final pat good-bye, even though I had to bite my lip to hold back, because it hurt so dreadful deep. Mr. Guthrie paid Dabney the cash, started his engine; we watched the truck smoke away the red sand of our road. As we watched it go Dab stood close to me and said, "I hate myself, Harry. If'n ya don't forgive me, I'll certain understand."

I didn't cry. Because nobody can cry empty.

"Come," said Dab.

165

With my arms still around Dab's chest, and my eyes tight shut, I felt my brother walking with me. The damp smell told me that we now stood inside our barn. I couldn't open my eyes or let loose of Dab. Like I'd never be able to stand alone again.

His strong arms held me close to him, and I didn't know who was shaking, my brother or me. Dab's shirt smelled of cows and sweat and ranch work, like it was a shirt he'd wore all his life without Poke's washing it. All I could do was kiss his shirt, again and again, to tell him that I was trying to understand.

Then I felt his cheek resting on my hair, and his sorrow falling down to my face, joining mine.

Chapter 26

September came.

I got up real early, as I'd been doing since Mama had took sick, and sneaked downstairs to fix her a breakfast tray. Our kitchen was still morning dusky.

A horse nickered. Looking out of the screen door, I saw Trudy Sue climbing off her sorrel mare. With her arms loaded with home-canned goods, she skipped up the steps; as I opened the door for her I noticed that she also had brought a fresh rose. It wasn't the first time Trudy Sue brought us jars of vegetables and pie fillings and stuff. She did it a lot.

"Thank you," I told her.

"My," she whispered to me, "you're up early. Where's your brother?"

"Asleep. He's wore out, like Mama."

Trudy Sue sighed. "I know." Then she smiled at me. "Here, this'll pretty up your mother's breakfast." She dropped the rose on the tray I was preparing, then unloaded the jars on a shelf near the window. She touched my face. "Soon," she said, "all of those sweet freckles will melt off. Maybe *you* won't miss seeing them, but I will."

"How soon?"

"Oh, sooner than a year or two. Well, maybe three. I can't stay, because Mother and I are still canning. All day long. So tell that brother of yours how glad I was to see *you* instead. Okay?"

"Sure."

"And remind him there's school tomorrow."

I shook my head. "Dab says he won't be going. Now that Mama's sick, he's gotta work the ranch."

Her face fell. "I understand, Harry. We'll all miss Dab at school."

I grinned at her and said, "You don't have to call me Harry no more. Because it's Harriet now. I'm twelve."

Trudy Sue left and was halfway to Goldie when she turned around and stopped. "You know," she told me, "from what I see and hear, Harriet Beecher, you're more than twelve. A lot more."

Smiling and waving, she mounted Goldie with a graceful swing of her leg and rode away. I went back to the stove to complete my mother's breakfast and then started to load up her tray. But I didn't have to tote it upstairs, because Mama appeared in her raggy red bathrobe.

"Mama?"

"I'm feeling powerful good today," she said, coming to me with a morning hug. "So I figured I just might brave it downstairs."

There seemed to be a bit more color in her cheeks, and noticing it sure did brighten my morning. "That's good," I told her. "Trudy Sue was here and brought you a rose for breakfast."

Touching the rose, then raising it to her nose, my mother helped herself to a whiff of fragrance. Moving it to my nose, she let me share its perfume. I told her that Trudy Sue brung it along with some jars of put-up food. Mama's soft smile told me how grateful she was.

"Dab's still asleep," she said. "I s'pose he'll be raging mad when he learns that he overslept and missed seeing his girl."

"Reckon so," I told her.

She looked at the tray and a plate of eggs and toast that I'd fixed for her. "My, that breakfast looks good enough to eat."

Mama sat at the kitchen table. I sat with her.

Outside, I heard the day's first argument, in the form of Poker and Lightning, who were strolling up from the bunkhouse. Though I couldn't catch every word, I concluded that the difference of opinion was over last evening's euchre.

My mother smiled. "Sounds normal."

The pair of them stomped up to the door, entered our kitchen, and then stared open-mouthed at Mama. For some reason, both Poker and Lightning yanked off their hats.

"Miz Beecher," said Poke, "it sure is a blessing to see you up for breakfast. Or rather *down*."

Lightning just grinned and nodded in his usual quiet way, then slid himself into a chair beside Mama. Poke, on the other hand, began to rattle around in the kitchen like he was fixing to feed the world. Or starve it.

"Where's Dab?" he snorted, abusing the stove as though it wasn't hot enough.

"I'm right here."

Turning my head, I saw Dabney, who was still in his pajamas, the knee of which was sporting a gaping rip.

"Best you toss those pajama pants in the mending basket," I ordered him in my bossiest voice.

He grinned at me. "Yes'm."

"Shucks," said Poker. "I can mend 'em up. What's one more chore on my list? Added to cooking, cleaning, sweeping out, and soaping the laundry." His voice sounded extra scratchy. "On top of all I got to handle."

The old man busied himself, breaking eggs into a black skillet, making a mess of it. Yellow dripped from his knotty old fingers. Then he turned to Dabney and me to bark out an order.

"Sit down, you two kids. And no dang complaining until breakfast gits ready."

Inside, I was itching to remind Poke that he was the only griper, but I held quiet, watching the old man spill coffee and burn bacon. He seemed to slap more butter on his apron than he did to the oven toast. He'd called us both *kids.* Well, to Poke, who had been here at Spanish Hoof since before either one of us got ourselfs hatched, Dabney and I would always be only that. Kids.

The five of us sat and forked in.

For a while back, we'd eaten our meals with only the four of us. Mama's chair had sat empty. But now we were five again. I watched Dabney surround his breakfast like he owned the hungriest belly in Florida. It sounded good.

Across the table, Lightning chewed slowly and quietly as compared to my brother. One of the strips of bacon on Lightning's plate was burnt black. He held it up to show Poker.

The old cook glowered at him. "I don't want to hear about it," Poke grunted.

"He cooks about as good as he plays cards," Lightning informed Mama.

Poker curled a lip at him, then turned to attack Dab. "You sure could use a barbering."

"No need," my brother answered with his mouth still chewing.

Pointing at Dab, the old man said, "In case you forgot, I always cut your hair on the day before school."

"I ain't going."

"How come?"

"Because I've learned it all."

Mama set down her white coffee mug, allowing it to rest on the faded blue oilcloth. "It'll be your decision, son," she said in a soft voice. "You proved you can make 'em." She looked at me. "Both of you have faced up to some bitter choices."

As she said it I knew that she meant my giving up Noble. Thinking about Mr. Guthrie's trucking away my pony caused Poke's breakfast to sort of hang halfway down my throat. Like I couldn't swallow no more.

"From now on," Mama continued to say, "if we're all to hold on, we best not fritter our time longing for what we lost. We gotta look to what begs doing."

"Yeah," said Poker. "I s'pose so." Yet his voice didn't sound too joyous. "Here," he said, taking Mama's mug, "let me top off your coffee, Miz Beecher. The pot's still got some."

Maybe, I was thinking, it was all we Beechers had left. One last sip of coffee. And then it just sort of blurted out. "I wonder what we actual *do* got left."

Dab looked at me. "We got us," he said.

Mama smiled.

"And we got Spanish Hoof," he said. "Last night I made us another decision. So listen up." His voice sounded deeper and strong. "I decided to take in two partners."

Poke frowned. "Who?"

Dabney grinned at the old man. "Oh, nobody real important. Just you and Lightning."

Poker's face wrinkled into a slow grin. "Ya mean it, Dab? Me'n Light? Does he mean it honest, Miz Beecher?"

"It's a grand idea," Mama said. "Because both

you hands asked to join in, a while back. So it was your request."

Poker grinned again. So did I.

"To give y'all the straight of it," Dab said, "we ain't got a whole smack of assets left. And we're up to our eyeballs in bills. But"—he looked at both Lightning and Poker—"if the two of ya still want to throw in with us, from now on, Spanish Hoof's got five owners. A five-way split."

"Okay with me," Lightning said.

"Me too," I added in, thinking how glad I felt that at last, in a strange new way, we finally were all Beechers.

Poke couldn't say a word. The old man just stood in the center of our kitchen, wiping his hands on his apron. But then he twirled around and booted the stove. "You're mine now, ya old black devil. Hear? So ya best behave. Or I'll kick ya from here to Yee-haw."

Dab wasn't through. "First off," he told us, "we'll meet last month's payment to the Otookee Bank from what we got by selling our animals."

Mama touched my hand.

"Then," he said, "we'll pay Hoolie Swain and Doc Strong. Using what Poke and Lightning kick in, I'm going to ask Mr. Ellsworth if I can buy us some wee little orange trees. Trudy Sue suggested it. She said that her daddy claims that citrus is going to be a lot bigger here in Florida than a lot of ranchers realize. Big as beef."

"I'll help," I told Dab.

He nodded at me. "You sure will."

Mama stood up. "I'd like," she said, "for all us wealthy partners to shake hands."

We did.

My hand held Mama's hand and Poke's big one; and it felt so clean good to know, as Dabney had earlier said, that still we had *us*. But there certain was plenty to do.

"Let's get to working," I said.

Chapter 27

I helped Poke.

Mama stayed indoors to go over some of our important papers. So Poker and I went to scatter cracked corn to the chickens, gather a few morning eggs, and sweep out the henhouse.

Poker, resting his broom to sneeze at the dust, looked at me. "Harry," he said, "I still can't git over the notion that you're hankering to be called Harriet." He shook his head. "How come?"

As I yanked dirty straw out of a laying box, stuffing in fresh, I told him. "Because I ain't eleven anymore." I wanted to inform Poker that lately I felt older than he was. But I didn't. Then a question itched me, so I asked it. "How old are you, Poke?"

Taking off his rumpled cowboy hat, the old man scratched his head. "Darned if I know. Years back, I quit counting."

"Maybe I will too," I said.

He looked out of the henhouse door. "Say, where did Light and Dabney go? I saw 'em hitch the mule to the wagon and head south."

"Dab said they were going to the Ellsworths'."

Poker winced. "To pay a social call on his good-looker gal, I s'pose."

"Well," I said, "maybe that too. Yet what they really went for was to buy us some little orange trees." Thinking about it made me a speck happier. Because it meant that Spanish Hoof would be growing again.

The old man snorted. "If'n ya ask me, there sure is a lot of drinks with a lot more personality than orange juice." Poke worked his mouth as though his throat was dry.

All I did was stare at him.

"Don't nag me," he grumbled. "For the last few Saturday nights we been to town, Light and me never even took one step in the direction of Nell's."

I shot him a firm nod of my head. But he doggone knew what I was telling him, without words. But then, just to make sure I'd nail it all down, I sang a line of the hymn we'd sung in church, on the Sunday morning when his head had been so hurtful: " 'Forgive me, Lord, forgive me.' "

The old man poked my ribs, playful like, with the butt end of his broom. "Harriet," he said, "you certain are a limit."

"Thanks," I said, smiling. "But I ain't a limit no longer. Let's get to work."

Later on, after Poker and I had shifted most of the henhouse dirt, or made a path through it, the old cook went to his kitchen. His absence gave me the chance to really clean out our henhouse and do it proper. Instead of hiding the chicken dirt, the way Poker done, I swept it all through the door.

It was nearing midafternoon when Dabney and Lightning returned, with Golly and a whole bunch of wispy green trees. Both men were walking to spare the mule.

"How many?" I asked Dab.

"Over six dozen," Dabney said, pulling the pins to let down the tailgate, to afford me a keener look. "We got sixty orange and the rest are grapefruit. Mr. Ellsworth give us a bargain price because these was all the runts of his recent shipment."

"Did you see Trudy Sue?"

Dab sighed. "Sort of. She and her ma was sweating in the kitchen, doing their canning. They must've had close to a hundred jars in boiling water, processing. And I learned one thing worth remembering."

"What was it?" I asked.

Dab shook his head. "When two steamy women are slicing, canning, and pouring wax in a hell-hot kitchen, they don't need me or Lightning in there too."

I helped Lightning unhitch Golly and carry her harness into the barn, to the tack room where we kept the saddles. Weeks and weeks ago, I'd cleared a peg in one corner to make a space for a someday pony saddle. The peg stuck out, vacant and alone.

We left our new citrus trees shaded in the wagon

because tomorrow, according to Dab, we'd start stretching out strings for the rows of our grove.

"Okay," I said. "And I'll help shovel out holes for the bags soon as I git off the school bus."

Dab sighed. "Never thought I'd say so," he said, "but I'm sorta going to miss high school. Seeing the gang and all."

It was then I realized that Dabney had given up things too. The same way I had to give up Noble. As he walked away I wanted to tell him so, yet I couldn't think of how to say it. Mama had near about given her whole strength to Spanish Hoof, so we'd have a home. And now Dabney was doing it.

"I'm glad you're my brother," I said in a whisper, even though he was standing too distant to hear.

Climbing up into the wagon bin, I examined some of our new trees up close. They were mostly runts, as my brother had said earlier. Yet one tree stood up a head or two taller than the rest. As I looked at it I spotted a tiny green ball.

"Dab!" I yelled. "We already got our first orange. Come see. Hurry!"

My brother looked at the one small green fruit and said, "Harriet, we're in the citrus business."

Poker come limping from the kitchen, to warn us that Mama, even though she'd got dressed, was napping on the parlor sofa, and for me to hush my noise. He then inspected the tiny green orange, which wasn't bigger than a marble.

"When's the big harvest?" Poke asked, in a voice

that sounded as if he was doubting there'd be one.

"Three or four years," Dab proudly told him. "And more every season—*partner.*"

Hearing it made Poker bend a grin. As Dabney walked away the old cook turned to me and spoke. "Ya don't gotta worry none about me 'n' Light wandering into Nell's Place. Joints like that are for hired hands. I'm a ranch *owner* now."

It sounded good to hear.

The late afternoon turned out to be a real September scorcher, and I noticed that some leaves on our citrus trees were starting to curl. So I borrowed Poke's old garden hose, hitched it to the spout beneath our windmill, and dragged the nozzle end almost to the wagon. The water pressure was just about enough to allow me to wet down the bagged trees that we'd purchased from Mr. Ellsworth.

Dabney and Lightning were passing by just as I was completing my watering job on our citrus trees. And I overheard my brother say something about me to Lightning that sort of pleased me some.

"Ya know," Dabney said, pointing my way, "there ain't one ounce of *quit* in that little package."

But the best part of the day come just after my brother and I milked Ruthie. We were pouring her warm milk into the giant can when I heard a noise that really sounded welcome. Without a word to Dab, I took off at a gallop, running as fast as I could across our south meadow. Maybe my brother hadn't heard the noise, yet I knew I certain could hear it.

"What's wrong?" Dabney was yelling.

I didn't answer.

Instead, my feet kept on running due south, to beyond a low clump of palmetto, where I pulled up for a breather. Most of what was left of our herd of brood cows was grazing a lot farther away, looking like a bunch of black dots. But not all of them. One cow stood nearby, her nose nudging a wet and shining newborn calf. Seeing it danced my heart.

The calf bawled again, making the sound I'd heard back yonder in our barn. Turning around, I yelled real loud.

"Dab! We got ourselfs a calf!"

I saw Dabney coming out of the barn, his hand over the brim of his hat, as though trying to learn why I was hollering at him. With a wave, I motioned for him to hurry.

"Come see, Dab!"

"Well, I'll be," he said when he final arrived to where I stood keeping a safe distance from the cow. "We got our first new drop."

"*Yahoo!*" I hooted.

Dab looked at me. "We're gonna hang on, girl. Spanish Hoof can make it prosperous again." His hand rested on my shoulder. "And maybe," he told me, "if we git a healthy new crop of calves, there might be some dough left, next year, for a new pony."

After he said it, I thought sudden about Noble and how wonderful he'd been. But I had something inside me to tell Dabney, so I let myself speak out. "I had me a pony. You're a good guy to offer it, but no thanks."

"How come, Harry?" Dab's entire face seemed to be one question.

"Because," I said, "I'm Harriet Beecher now. And I aim to be a partner too. Not just a little kid on a pony ride. Maybe it's time *you* an' *me* ate a chicken wing, the way Mama always does." As I spoke I was hoping Dabney would understand what I was trying so hard to say. Because not even wanting a pony could stand in the way of our holding on to Spanish Hoof.

Dab couldn't seem to say anything. All he did was wrap his arms around me as we stood there on our own land, watching the cow lick her calf, feeling the strong Florida sun.

And the warm of each other.

ROBERT NEWTON PECK comes from a long line of farmers. Like the people he most often writes about, he was raised in the country way, in rural Vermont. Since the publication of *A Day No Pigs Would Die,* he has written thirty-eight books and has won millions of fans with the spirited escapades of Soup and Rob, who also starred in three ABC After-School Specials.

He is the winner of the 1982 Mark Twain Award and lives in Longwood, Florida, but he often travels to schools and colleges, where he talks about writing and books and plays ragtime piano.